ONCE UPON A TIME IN TITTYBONG 2

Once Upon a Time in Tittybong 2

Catch My Disease

SIMON SHERIDAN

Simon Sheridan

Contents

Chapter 1

"JJ, you've got a customer."

Krusty held open the front door of the house and a young blonde woman flashed him a smile as she walked into the lounge room to find JJ crumpled up on the couch in a posture that resembled a pile of clothes with a wig thrown on top. His face was scarcely visible beneath his shoulder-length mouse brown hair which was normally pulled back behind his ears but which now formed a kind of curtain through which his nose protruded like the snorkel of a scuba diver. The girl stood a few metres away from the couch and waited for signs of life but none were forthcoming. Krusty cleared his throat and closed the door extra loud as if that might wake his friend. When he saw that it didn't, he walked over to the couch and prodded JJ with his foot the way a would-be customer might kick the tyres of a second-hand car.

"Oi! Anybody home?"

JJ emitted a sound that was part murmur, part grumble and part gargle. He turned himself over so that his back was now facing the room.

"Hangover?" asked the woman looking towards the couch with a measure of pity.

"Worse," said Krusty.

"Drugs?"

Krusty shook his head.

"What then?"

"Girls."

"Oh, right. Amber," said the girl as the slow dawn of comprehension spread over her face. It was quickly replaced by a querulous look.

"But they broke up ages ago."

"Over a month," said Krusty.

"And he's still heartbroken? Awww, that's cute."

"Pathetic is what it is," said Krusty loudly in the direction of the couch.

"How did they break up?"

"She dumped him. Dumped him like a sack of potatoes."

This finally got a rise out of JJ who turned over into an upright position on the couch. He looked like he hadn't slept for days and his bloodshot eyes would have been more fitting on a Friday night smoking some of Krusty's produce rather than a Monday morning.

"She didn't dump me," he said rubbing his hands over his face as if trying to wake himself up.

"Yay, he's finally up and about," said Krusty clapping his hands in faux enthusiasm. "That's the most energetic I've seen him in a month."

"She didn't dump me," repeated JJ.

"Ok, fine. She didn't dump you. You've got a customer, bro. Look, it's Phoebe."

JJ lifted his eyes and the blank, distant expression gave way to a flash of recognition.

"Hi, Phoebe," he said feigning a smile.

"Hi," said Phoebe waving and smiling in an uncertain fashion as if JJ was a wild animal who might do something unexpected at any moment.

"What are you after?" asked JJ hauling himself up from the couch and lumbering towards the bedroom at the front of the house which constituted the storeroom for his inventory.

"A phone. Pink, if you've got one," said Phoebe.

Mobile phones were JJ's stock in trade but he also sold televisions and stereos as well as various computer parts and other random electrical gadgets. The last of the electrical goods stores had shut up shop in Tittybong two years prior but it wasn't until the department store in the neighbouring town of Bong Bong closed that business for JJ really took off. To buy a new phone or television, a resident of Tittybong now had to travel over two hundred kilometres each way. Even if they had the patience for such a trip, there were few people left who could afford the luxury of buying new. A second-hand gadget was all most people could expect and JJ had rightfully earned his reputation for quality. His main point of differentiation from his competitors was the simple fact that he knew his way around a soldering iron and had the basic tools and knowledge to make things work as opposed to the shady characters on street corners who could barely be bothered to plug a unit into a wall socket to check that it was functional before flogging it off to the highest bidder. Between the sales of functional second-hand devices and the repair of existing ones, JJ had grown himself a thriving business quite by accident and, although the operation was in what you might call a grey zone from a legal and taxation standpoint, the powers-that-be had so far left him alone and his customers even included some local notables who, for reasons of propriety, sent their business through intermediaries. Phoebe was one of his long-term customers. She had a nice habit of losing phones and breaking devices and she came from a wealthy family in the city which meant replacing them was not the financial burden it might have been for others.

"All I've got are hot pink or this kind of pinky-purple," said JJ emerging from the bedroom and holding up two phones.

"I'll take the hot pink."

JJ handed her the phone and Phoebe inspected its condition.

"The crack in the screen here is pretty big," she said pointing to the bottom left corner of the phone.

"I don't have any non-cracked screens in that model," said JJ curtly. "I can give you a different phone with a better screen but not in pink."

Phoebe thought about it for a few seconds.

"Alright," she said letting out a long sigh. "I'll take it."

"That'll be a hundred and twenty dollars. I've taken thirty off because of the screen."

"Right. Well, that's the other thing I needed to talk to you about," said Phoebe looking at JJ with a sheepish expression. "The problem is, I don't have any cash."

This time it was JJ who let out a sigh. In his line of business this refrain was so common that he'd installed a sign on the wall of the lounge room. It was one of those old novelty signs and it read "CA$H ONLY". He pointed to it as he spoke.

"Sorry, Phoebe, we don't do credit here."

"No, no, no," said Phoebe anxious to clarify. "I've got the money. I just can't get hold of the cash."

JJ hadn't heard this particular excuse before. He furrowed his brow trying to parse its meaning and Phoebe could see that she needed to explain further.

"As you probably know, the government in Sydney has put a freeze on the bank accounts of all public servants. Well, it's not really a freeze. It's just that they can no longer withdraw cash. All receipts and payments have to be made electronically from now on. Apparently, they're going to do the same to everybody's account in about six months."

"I've heard about this shit," said Krusty who had been rolling himself a joint by the kitchen table. "They're trying to get rid of cash. That might be a problem for the, ummm, thingo."

Krusty made a vague gesture towards the CA$H ONLY sign before flicking on his zippo and taking a long toke on the joint.

"I don't understand what a cash freeze on bureaucrats in Sydney has to do with selling a mobile phone in Tittybong," said JJ.

"I get most of my money from my father who works for the government. If he can't get cash, then he can't send me any cash," said Phoebe.

"Well, can't he transfer it somebody else's account and they can send you the cash?"

"The government is tracking all transfers now so they can follow where the money is going."

"Again, I don't see how this is my problem."

"It's going to become your problem soon," said Phoebe. "In six months, there's not going to be any more cash. They're starting with the public servants but they are going to roll out the cash ban to everybody. How are you going to run a cash only business when that happens?"

JJ realised Phoebe had a point. Even in the short term, the cash ban on public servants would be a problem as many of his customers could only afford luxuries like mobile phones due to money sent from relatives in the city. This would mean a sharp drop in sales which would only be exacerbated once the full cash ban came into effect. The more he thought about it, the more he realised a cash ban represented an existential threat to his and Krusty's livelihoods. Krusty's main business was weed and that was all cash too. You certainly couldn't put *dope* down in the description of an electronic transfer.

"When did all this start?" asked JJ.

"About two weeks ago," answered Phoebe.

"So, that's why business has been slow lately," observed Krusty.

"I didn't notice."

"That's cos you've been lying on the couch dreaming about Amber," said Krusty.

JJ let out a long sigh and began pacing up and down the room.

"Alright, well, let's think about the situation. If people can only transfer money electronically, then I guess we need to get a bank account. But even if we could find a bank that would give us an account, any transfers to it would leave a paper trail and that's not going to work for our line of business."

"Don't you have, I dunno, *associates* or something that can make paper trails disappear?" asked Phoebe.

"Money launderers," suggested Krusty.

"Exactly. Do you know any money launderers?"

"I don't think so," said JJ.

"Dude, of course we do," said Krusty.

"Who?"

"Macbeth."

"Woah, you guys know Macbeth?" exclaimed Phoebe.

"We don't know him," said JJ, "but we do business with the Macbeth Corporation."

"They must do a lot of money laundering, right?"

"Dude, their whole business would have to be laundered."

"Ok. But that doesn't mean they will launder our money."

"It's worth finding out, isn't it?" asked Phoebe.

"What I don't understand is how this is going to work for the broader community," said JJ continuing his pacing. "I mean, doesn't the money supply come from the government? If the government stops providing the money, how is anybody in Tittybong going to get cash?"

"It depends on what the federal government does with all the cash that's not in use in the cities. Will they burn it? Will it they allow it to be released outside of the cities?" said Phoebe.

"Dude, we should totally start our own bank," said Krusty taking one last toke on his joint before putting it out in the ashtray on the kitchen bench.

"That's a brilliant idea," said Phoebe. "There hasn't been a bank in Tittybong for years."

"We'll call it The People's Bank of Tittybong."

"Hah! That's a great name," said Phoebe giving Krusty a high five.

"I think you two are getting a little ahead of yourselves. We don't even know if we can get any money yet and you're already starting a bank," said JJ grumpily.

"Well, let's go and see Snake now, bro," said Krusty.

"Who's Snake?" asked Phoebe.

"He's our main contact with Macbeth. We can ask him about the laundering idea."

JJ gave another long sigh. He didn't like the sound of the idea but he didn't have any other ideas that were better.

"Alright. It can't hurt to go and ask the question," he said finally.

"Excellent," said Krusty slapping JJ on the shoulder. "We've finally got you off the couch and back in action, bro."

JJ muttered something and went hunting for the keys to his motorbike.

"Hey, what about the phone?" asked Phoebe who held up the hot pink phone she had chosen.

"Oh, yeah. Tell you what, I'll let you take it for now while we organise payment," said JJ. "But just this once and only for you. Don't tell anybody else about it."

"Thanks, Jay," said Phoebe giving him a kiss on the cheek as she headed for the door.

"Gimme a call when you know what's happening with the bank transfer," she sang out as the screen door slapped shut behind her.

Krusty walked over to the sideboard and picked up a set of keys which he threw over to JJ.

"Let's hit the road, bro."

***

Macbeth's full name was Pickles Macbeth, although it is to be doubted that this was either the moniker bestowed on him by his parents or recorded on his birth certificate in the unlikely event such a document existed. What little was known about Macbeth was entirely transmitted via gossip and innuendo. Some people claimed to have seen him but no photograph confirmed his existence, a strange fact given that mobile phones with cameras were still ubiquitous throughout most of Australia including the no-go zones outside the big cities. Rumour had it that anybody caught in possession of a camera around Macbeth could expect a quick and not necessarily painless demise. Such a threat was credible. Macbeth's operatives were everywhere including the big cities. In fact, a large part of Macbeth's business was facilitating the black market trade between the cities and the rest of the country.

Macbeth's business had grown in direct proportion to the withdrawal of government from large parts of the country. This process had been happening for some time as politicians focused on integrating the cities with the globalist network that linked most of the western world while leaving the rest of the country to its own devices. The effect was felt firstly in the lack of services provided. Little things like libraries and recreation centres disappeared. Then there was a lack of money for things like police and medical personnel and finally a lack of governance altogether. This all happened so slowly that nobody really noticed but the process had created a void and into that void had stepped a number of entrepreneurial souls providing the functions formerly fulfilled by the state. One of those entrepreneurial souls was Pickles Macbeth. Among the services offered by the Macbeth Corporation were "transportation", which was less about trucking and logistics and more about ensuring the contents being trucked and logisticked actually arrived at their destination. Debt collection was a booming business as were the traditional staples of the mob boss: money laundering and drug trafficking.

It was the latter which had brought JJ and Krusty into contact with the Macbeth Corporation about a year earlier. Some of Krusty's homegrown weed, which was already legendary in the Tittybong area, had found its way to Sydney where a Macbeth associate had been so impressed with the quality that he ordered an investigation into its origins. A couple of days later, two large men on motorcycles pulled up in front of the rundown house where JJ and Krusty lived and offered to buy as much weed as they could produce. For JJ and Krusty, newly graduated from school with no job prospects to speak of, it was an offer too good to refuse. The success of the drug enterprise later expanded into JJ's electrical goods business. Another of the Macbeth Corporation's verticals was second-hand (read: stolen) goods and JJ began on-selling these to people like Phoebe. The two businesses proved symbiotic. They would transport Krusty's weed to Sydney and return with used mobile phones, televisions and the other devices that JJ would then fix up and offer for sale in Tittybong. This had proved lucrative enough that JJ and Krusty now owned motorbikes and it was those bikes which rumbled into the front yard of an old factory on the outskirts of Sydney near the suburb of Liverpool. The factory was one of Macbeth's main distribution centres and was Krusty and JJ's primary point of contact with the Corporation.

They parked their bikes and walked into the office via the glass door at the side of the factory. An old brown leather couch, a couple of plastic chairs and a raggedly wooden coffee table constituted a small waiting area to the right as you entered. Immediately to the left was the reception desk behind which sat a young woman dressed in the style of what would once have been called *punk rock* which had become the de facto standard among Macbeth Corporation associates. The bottom part of her head was shaved revealing several small tattoos which the long jet-black hair emanating from the top of her head did not hide. There were more tattoos to be found lower on her body. In fact, the entire area from the side of her head, down her neck and to the end of the arm was covered in them creating a rather confronting appearance which was off-set by the friendly smile she gave the two young men as they entered.

"Well, well, well, if it isn't my favourite country bumpkins."

"Is that all we are to you, Ciara? Bumpkins?" said Krusty walking over to the counter.

"Nah. Sometimes I think of you as just plain old rednecks."

"Well, I love you too. And just to show how much, I've bought you a present."

Krusty hoisted the large black plastic bag that he had carried into the office onto the small table beside the reception desk.

"Another batch of Krusty's Special?"

"Five kilograms worth," said Krusty patting the bag.

"I suppose you want me to process this for you now?"

"If you don't mind, sugar plum," grinned Krusty.

Ciara gave an involuntary chortle as she got out of her chair and picked up the bag.

"Back in a minute, *darl*-ing" she said as she lugged the bag down the small corridor to the left of the counter.

"Hey, Ciara. Can you tell Snake we want to see him".

"Alright. Take a seat and I'll see if he's free".

Krusty flopped himself down on the couch and JJ sat in one of the plastic chairs.

"Whaddya think of Ciara?" asked Krusty turning his head to JJ.

"She's cute," said JJ.

"Reckon I'd be in with a shot?"

"Sure."

"I might ask her to come for a drink later. Hey, maybe she can bring a friend along for you."

Krusty slapped his friend playfully on the thigh but JJ was staring off into space.

"Don't tell me you're still thinking about Amber."

"No. I'm thinking about the future of our town and the future of us," said JJ turning to his friend with a stern look. "You do understand the gravity of the situation, don't you? We might be out of business soon and who knows whether Tittybong will even exist in a year if there's no money supply."

"C'mon, bro. It's not that bad. We'll figure something out. You just need to have a night on the town. Let's go into the city and check out that pub we went to last time. What was it called, The Goat's Horns?"

"The Ram's Head," corrected JJ.

"Yeah. Let's go there. Have a few beers. Meet some girls. Take your mind off the worries of the world for a night."

JJ was about to respond when a man appeared at the end of the small corridor walking towards them. As per his name, he had a large snake tattoo on his forearm and was dressed in the black leather motorcycle gear that was common for Macbeth associates. This was partly a fashion statement but mostly a practical necessity as the motorcycle was the preferred method of transport in the Corporation. Although Snake was only in his mid to late twenties, he was known as one of Macbeth's closest advisors and was the manager the distribution centre among other things. He carried a manila folder in his hand which he threw onto the coffee table in front of JJ.

"I assume this is what you're after, Mr JJ," he said.

JJ looked at the folder with confusion which was briefly replaced by recognition and then a kind of embarrassment.

He started to lean forward as if to collect the folder and then changed his mind preferring instead to try and change the subject.

"Actually, Snake, we're here about another matter..." he began before Krusty, with an infallible sixth sense for the discomfort of his friend, sat up on the couch, swept up the folder and began leafing through its contents.

JJ jumped up and attempted to snatch the folder away but Krusty turned his back leaving his friend helplessly lodged between the couch and the coffee table in a fruitless attempt to reach over Krusty's shoulder. To make matters even worse, Ciara returned to the room just in time to see the kerfuffle.

"What's all this?" she asked.

Krusty held up a large A4 photograph. It was a close-up picture of a scantily clad pretty young blonde woman taken through what looked to be her bedroom window. Ciara took a step forward and craned her neck to get a better look.

"Who's that?" she asked as Krusty weaved around JJ's flailing outstretched hand to give her the photo.

"Wow. She's beautiful," said Ciara studying the picture.

"That's JJ's ex-girlfriend Amber. The one he's still pining over."

"I can see why."

"I'm not pining over her," said JJ who made another lunge for the folder that Krusty was holding only to knock it out of his hand and have the contents, perhaps thirty photos in total, spill out over the floor. The photos showed Amber in various locations including her bedroom, drinking a coffee at the local café and working out at a gym.

"That looks less like pining and more like stalking," said Krusty and as he watched JJ scramble to gather up the photos.

"One of our agents in Sydney has been doing the stalking on his behalf," said Snake. "Just another little service offered by the Corporation."

"What he needs is a dating service," said Krusty.

"That's one thing that we don't offer," said Snake. "There's more money in stalking."

"I'll bet."

"Don't listen to them, JJ," said Ciara who handed the photo of Amber back to JJ. "I think it's sweet that you're in love with a girl enough to pine for her. None of the guys around here would do that."

"I'd pine for you if we broke up, Ciara," said Krusty with a wink.

"In order to break up, we'd first have to be going out."

"Oh?"

Having finally sorted the photos and papers back into the folder, JJ threw it down on the coffee table with a thud as if to bring the discussion to an end.

"This is not what we came here for," said JJ turning around to face Snake with a flushed expression on his face.

"So, what did you come for? Apart from dropping off another bag of Krusty's Special."

Snake gave a respectful nod in Krusty's direction who returned the favour.

"We came here because we want to know if one of the other services you offer is money laundering. We want to be able to have money transferred to a bank account and then withdraw the cash without the authorities tracing it."

"This wouldn't have anything to do with the new cash ban on certain accounts in Sydney, would it?" asked Snake with a knowing grin.

"Maybe," said JJ not knowing whether it was better to tell the truth or not and doing neither and both at the same time.

"You're about tenth person today to call looking for cash, my friend. Unfortunately, the rules have now changed within the Corporation due to the change in circumstances and we are no longer able to be so liberal with cash payments. Speaking of cash payments, here you go K-man. For the weed."

Snake threw a small wad of cash to Krusty who caught it with a smile.

"Thanks, bro."

"So, you'll still be paying in cash?" asked JJ.

"Of course. The cash ban is just for government employees and, in case you haven't noticed, the Macbeth Corporation is not a part of the government."

"But what about when the cash ban is rolled out to everybody in the city. Will you still be paying in cash then?"

"That's classified information, I'm afraid. Let's just say the Corporation will be making arrangements to ensure business can still be conducted so you've got nothing to worry about there."

"That's fine for the corporation," said JJ, "but what about Tittybong? What about other towns like Tittybong? How is the money supply going to work in those kinds of places?"

"That's your problem," shrugged Snake.

"No, it's an opportunity. There are three and half thousand people in Tittybong alone. All of them rely on cash in one way or another. That's an awful lot of cash moving around that somebody can profit from and last time I checked the Macbeth Corporation was interested in profit."

JJ left a pregnant pause and allowed the rising intonation of his final sentence to serve as an invitation to continue.

"Alright, I'm listening," said Snake.

"Here's how it could work," explained JJ. "Almost everybody in town will still need to transact with banks in the city. So, we'd need to have a single account that we can tell them to transfer to. The systems would need to be conducted in such a way that the transactions cannot be traced but I'm sure the Macbeth Corporation knows how to do that already. For providing these services, we charge a fee on a per transaction basis. It would be just like a bank."

"The People's Bank of Tittybong," interjected Krusty.

"That's a great name and a great idea," laughed Ciara.

They looked over to see what Snake's reaction was and, after a few seconds of deliberation, he nodded his head sagely.

"Not bad. Pretty good for a couple of hillbillies."

"We prefer to be called bumpkins, dude," said Krusty flashing a cheeky smile at Ciara.

"So, what do you think, Snake? Can we make this happen?" asked JJ expectantly.

Snake looked JJ and Krusty up and down like a bank manager evaluating a customer for a loan.

"Alright, here's the deal," he said finally. "The cash thing is just the tip of the iceberg. There's a whole raft of changes coming soon that are going to upend pretty much everything about the status quo in this country. I'll give you just one example. The walls of Sydney," Snake gestured to the north where only a couple of kilometres away the large sandstone wall that had been under construction for about ten years stood, "they're going to be closed permanently to external visitors starting in two weeks. Oh, and the general cash ban, that's not happening in six months. It's happening much sooner. They're gonna pull the whole thing off in one go."

"Who's *they*?" asked Krusty.

"The Global Council."

"The global what?"

"You don't know the Global Council? You two really are a couple of hillbillies."

"I know the Global Council," said JJ glumly. "Amber's father is a member."

"That's right," said Snake. "Which is what made it so easy to get photos of your girlfriend, Mr JJ. We already had a couple of men watching her father."

"Hang on, you were dating the Prime Minister's daughter?" asked Ciara.

"I didn't know she was his daughter until we broke up," shrugged JJ.

"Does anybody wanna tell me what the Global Council is?" asked Krusty.

"The Global Council are the peak international governing body. They pretty much run this country now. Well, they run the cities. They're not too interested in the countryside. That's why they're bringing in the cash ban and the closing of the city walls. They reckon it will make thing easier to manage," said Snake.

"What does it mean that the city gates are closing?" asked JJ.

"Only registered travellers with permits will be allowed to enter and leave."

"This is bad. All the people in Tittybong will be cut off from their family in the city."

"Fear not, my friend. The Macbeth Corporation will be offering a new service to get people in and out of the cities. For a fee, of course."

Snake gave a wink.

"Well, what about a fee for the bank idea. Can we make that happen? It would be worth your while financially, wouldn't it?"

"That's what I was getting at. The Macbeth Corporation is aware of what is going on and we have a plan to deal with the developments including the cash ban. I can't tell you what the plan is. That's top secret. But I can tell you that part of the plan involves an alternative supply of cash."

"Including for Tittybong?"

"Maybe."

"Maybe?"

"As I said, I can't reveal any details."

"Then just let us handle the Tittybong part of the business. You'll need somebody to run it, won't you?"

"As I said earlier, the rules around this kind of thing are tightening up. Only certified associates of the corporation will be allowed to run something like that from now on."

"Then make us certified associates of the corporation."

"What he means is, you'll need to become fully initiated members of the Macbeth Corporation," said Ciara. "It's not just some form you fill out. It's a little bit more, ummm, physical in nature. Is that something you are willing to go through with?"

"Are you a member, Ciara?" asked Krusty.

"Sure am," said Ciara pointing to a spot just below her shoulder where a tattoo of the Macbeth insignia was placed.

"Well, then sign us up, dudes."

"It's not that simple. You have to agree to the rules of the corporation including strict loyalty to Macbeth."

"Fine by me," said Krusty.

"And there's an initiation process to go through," smiled Ciara.

"As a way to prove your loyalty to the Corporation," added Snake with a grin.

"Is it long?"

"No. In fact, it's very short."

"Short and, errr, *sweet*."

"We could do it this afternoon," said Ciara.

"That quickly?"

"There's just happens to be an all-Corporation meeting this afternoon. We normally do inductions as part of that. What do you think, Snake?"

Ciara raised a querying eyebrow towards Snake who still looked unconvinced.

"This is all a bit quick for my liking. But I will admit these boys have shown initiative and have been reliable contractors of the Corporation for some time. Not to mention the fact that we do need some new members to run these new programs. I want to be very clear, though, if you agree to come this afternoon you will witness secrets of the Macbeth Corporation that are never to be spoken about with anybody else. Even the likes of Amber," Snake gestured towards the manila folder. "Even your own mother. Am I understood? This is not the Boy Scouts you're joining here. The punishment for breaking the oath of silence is death."

Snake's tone of voice which, until now had been light hearted and jovial, took on a deep and deadly serious resonance that, combined with a piercing gaze from his pale blue eyes, caused JJ's stomach to twist. Krusty, however, seemed unperturbed.

"Sure, bro. We can keep a secret."

"JJ?"

"Just give us a minute to talk it over," said JJ as he motioned to Krusty to follow him outside where he led him away from the office door and over near their bikes.

"This is not the kind of thing we should be rushing into. We're talking about joining the mob here not the local football club," he said in a hushed tone even though there was nobody else around.

"Yeah, and you heard what Snake said about the cash ban and other stuff. Shit's getting real, bro, and it's about to kick off in a matter of weeks, not months."

"I'd rather have some time to think about it."

"We don't have time. Besides, if the money is about to run out, wouldn't you like to be the one holding it rather than the one begging for it? Those are the options in front of us, bro. Unless you've got a third alternative?"

"No, I don't."

"Dude, we've just hit the jackpot. We're about to become the fuckin' bank. Couple of percent per transaction just for moving money from A to B. We'll be rolling in it."

"I don't like the sound of this initiation ceremony."

"Like Snake said, it'll be quick. We'll probably just have to pledge allegiance to the flag and all that shit."

JJ thought about it for a few more seconds but realised that Krusty was right. It did seem like a better idea to be the ones handling the cash at a time like this.

"Alright," said JJ letting out a long sigh. "I don't like it but I think you're right. Let's do it."

"Good decision, bro."

They walked back inside where Snake and Ciara were looking at something behind the reception desk.

"I just wanna confirm one thing, Snake," said JJ. "If we join, you'll let us run the banking for the Tittybong area. Can we make that part of the deal?"

"No problem, Mr JJ."

"Ok. Count us in."

Snake gave a nod to Ciara who walked over and opened the top drawer on the other side of the desk. She removed two pieces of black cloth and walked over behind JJ from where she proceeded to strap what turned out to be a blindfold around his eyes tying it securely behind his head. When she was satisfied that it was on properly, she walked over behind Krusty and repeated the process.

"Are you gonna tie me up too or does that happen later?" asked Krusty.

"Only if you're lucky," giggled Ciara.

"What's involved in this initiation ceremony?" asked JJ.

"It's better if you don't know," smiled Ciara as she stepped away from Krusty and confirmed that the blindfolds were attached correctly.

"Alright, gentlemen," said Snake. "We've got about a half an hour drive ahead of us. From this point forward you are bound by the rules of the Macbeth Corporation and any transgressions of the rules will be punished so I suggest you keep those blindfolds exactly where they are and sit tight until we reach our destination. It'll all be over before you know it and you'll soon be the newest Macbeth associates. Let's go."

***

It was when the large man in the black leather outfit showed up holding a pink dressing gown and matching shower cap that JJ knew things were about to get weird. They had already heard the chanting and cheering through the metal walls of the meat locker in which Snake and Ciara had left them about an hour earlier. It resembled a distant football crowd. Snake and Ciara had now returned with the large man. They wore the kinds of silly grins on their faces of people who are about to play a practical joke but are trying not to give the game away. Snake told JJ and Krusty to strip down to their underwear and put on the pink bathrobes and shower caps. After a period of grumbling, they had acquiesced to the command. The large man then handed them the final piece of the outfit: a pair of pink slippers with fluffy white bonbons on the front.

"Absolutely outstanding," laughed Snake as the two men in pink stood before him with scowls of disapproval on their faces. "Alright, gentlemen, follow us."

Snake and Ciara walked ahead and JJ and Krusty followed them out of the room into a wide hallway with concrete floors and painted white walls that reflected the neon glare from the fluorescent lights above. They passed several rooms identical to the one they had just left before exiting the corridor into a large open space that had the feel of an underground pub or club. There was a bar over by the wall to their left, a couple of pool tables in the middle and some pinball machines on the right. Straight ahead was the large crowd that had been making all the noise. There must have been several hundred people clad almost entirely in black leather. They were standing in front of a large stage with PA system. Snake brought them to a halt at the back of the crowd just near the pool tables.

Somebody was talking on the stage and whatever they said caused a cheer from the crowd who all raised their right arm with the index finger pointing straight to the sky which seemed like some kind of symbolic gesture. As the crowd put their arms back down again, JJ got a glimpse of the stage for the first time and realised that the voice coming through the PA was from a young girl who was talking into a microphone. She had brown pigtails hanging down from either side of her face and was wearing a long black dress. The expression on her face was of intense seriousness and when she spoke it was with an authority that belied her age and the high-pitched tone of her voice. It was as if an army general or a police commander had been transported into the body of a small girl.

"Who's that?" asked JJ turning to Snake.

"That's Macbeth," he replied.

"What the fuck?" exclaimed Krusty.

"That's Macbeth?" said JJ. "The infamous crime boss who controls the black market in half of the country is a young girl?"

"You didn't know that?" asked Snake with a smile and a raised eyebrow.

"No, I didn't know that."

"Well, now you know. Pipe down. She's coming to the end of her speech and then it'll be your time to shine."

Macbeth removed the microphone from its stand and began prowling the stage like an angry panther.

"There are other logistical changes that you will be informed about in due course. For now, I wish only to impress upon you, comrades, the importance of this moment which represents a decisive turning point in our fight against the globalist scum. They no longer even pretend to govern this country. They are happy to leave anybody outside of the cities to fend for themselves. Their single purpose is to extract from this land what they want with no care for culture or the good of society. Their greed is our strength, comrades. Their weakness our opportunity. We will plant our flag where they fear to tread and we will pick them off from within while we build our forces without. When the time comes, and come it will, we shall strike the final dagger into their dark hearts and vanquish the evil from this land. Are you with me, comrades?"

A boisterous cheer went up from the audience – "yeah!"

"Are you with me comrades?" intoned the diminutive figure crossing to the other side of the stage.

"Yeah!"

"It is time, comrades. What is it time for?"

"Slay Duncan!"

"What is it time for?"

"Slay Duncan!"

"One more time, comrades!" shouted the young girl lifting her right index figure to the sky.

The crowd lifted its right index figure to the sky and at an earth shaking volume intoned – "Slay Duncan!"

The crowd broke out into delirious applause and Macbeth stood at the front of the stage with a satisfied look on her face. After a time, she put the microphone back into the stand and the noise gradually tapered off.

"Dude, who the fuck is Duncan?" asked Krusty.

"I dunno," shrugged JJ. "Maybe he's one of the globalists or something."

"There is no Duncan," snapped Snake, who had overheard the question. "Slay Duncan is the slogan for the Corporation and in future you two will need to join in the chant instead of standing there slobbering like a couple of lost dogs."

"We weren't slobbering."

"Quiet. It's almost time."

There was a large chair which JJ realised was actually a throne in the centre of the stage. Macbeth jumped on it and swung around so she was seated with her legs dangling down over the front. A man walked over to the microphone.

"Comrades, we will now move to the final order of business for the evening. An initiation for two new members who wish to join the Corporation."

The audience, seeming to know the drill by heart, immediately began to part in the middle forming a corridor which led straight back to where JJ and Krusty were standing. JJ's heart began to beat faster at the several hundred sets of eyes which were focused on him as he stood there in his pink bathrobe, shower cap and slippers.

"Let's go," said Snake giving JJ and Krusty a nudge on the shoulder to signal for them to walk in front of him through the middle of the crowd. A sea of faces, some bearded, some tattooed, mostly smirking and many leering greeted JJ who resolved to look straight ahead and try not to pay attention but this just made him realise that he was shaking in the knees as if one little push would be all it would take to send him crumbling to the floor.

"Got some fresh meat, have we, Snake?"

"Lambs to the slaughter."

"Better get the meat hooks ready."

These were some of the more family friendly taunts that rang out as they made their way through the crowd. Snake acknowledged the joviality with a ceremonial nod and led JJ and Krusty to the front of the stage and then over to the right where they ascended several stairs up onto the stage proper. He placed them on the right hand side a metre or two back from the front. JJ surveyed the leather-clad crowd. It consisted mostly of men you wouldn't want to meet in a dark alley at night. There seemed to be more tattoos than skin on display and there were quite a lot of weapons tucked into leather holsters. One positive, at least from the point of view of a young man, was the rather high proportion of women in the crowd although they were not the kind of girls one would meet in Tittybong. They followed Ciara in having a strong attachment to piercings and silver jewellery as a complement to black leather and their hairstyles alternated between short and spiky and long and complicated. The crowd was young. They were mostly around JJ's age with just a couple of older folk in the room.

Without any overt signal from anywhere, the crowd began chanting and the chanting got gradually louder as another man ascended the stage from the stairs on the side opposite JJ and Krusty. JJ looked over to see that he was dressed in an identical outfit except rather than being pink, his bathrobe, shower cap and slipper combination was a bright yellow. The man was one of the older people in the room and would have been in his fifties or sixties with a large beer belly not hidden by the bathrobe and a long white beard. He looked a little like a yellow version of Santa Claus and he held a clipboard ceremonially in his right hand as he took up a position at the front of the stage opposite JJ and Krusty. The yellow Santa Claus held up his hand to the crowd and the room became silent before his bellowing voice, which did not need any further amplification from the PA system, rang out like a town crier.

"Comrades, do you see these vile, scum-sucking vermin here before you?" he said gesturing to JJ and Krusty on the other side of the stage.

"Yeah!" shouted the crowd.

"Do you see these two despicable low-lifes, these repulsive, revulsive, abhorrent and obnoxious abominations?

"Yeah!"

"Let us enquire of these odious, nauseating wretches, what is their purpose here."

There was silence in the room as all faces turned to JJ and Krusty who stood with mystified looks on their faces as the crowd eyed them off expectantly.

"Dude, are we supposed to say something?" whispered Krusty out of the corner of his mouth.

"I dunno," said JJ under his breath.

"Vermin, why are you here?" screamed the man in yellow this time turning his head towards the two to make it clear who he was referring to.

"Umm, we're here to join the Corporation, bro," said Krusty.

"Do you hear that, Comrades? These puss-eating skelfs, these dung-munching nudniks want to join the Corporation. What say you to this request?"

The crowd erupted into booing and whistling. JJ once again felt his knees weaken as pointed fingers, waved fists and angry tongues were hurled in his direction. He wondered whether he and Krusty were about to be eaten alive. After a time, the man in yellow once again held up his hand for silence. JJ looked over and realised that he was reading off a piece of paper on the clipboard.

"The crowd has spoken. Who here speaks for the vermin?"

"I do," said Snake from the side of the stage and he lifted his arm in the familiar gesture with index finger pointing to the sky.

"What say you in their favour, comrade?"

Snake began to speak and JJ noticed that he too was reading from a script but one that he held in a small bit of paper in his hand.

"Comrades, these two who stand before you are the most repugnant, loathsome and detestable worms on the face of this earth. These yucky, yellow-bellied yahoos have been retrieved straight from the pits of abomination and brought before you tonight. I abhor, detest and despise them. I disown them."

Having played his part, Snake took a step back and tucked the paper into his pant pocket. The crowd proceeded to once again go apeshit until the man in yellow called for silence. He held up his hand as if trying to placate the angry mob.

"Comrades, we are here on a mission of mercy. These miserable wretches, now disowned by their only friend, throw themselves upon the bosom of your charity. Will you accept their desperate cry?"

This time there was no response from the crowd.

"Comrades, will you offer these strays a cup of the milk of human kindness wherewith to quench the thirst of their desire?"

A handful of shouts that sounded more of less positive and a smattering of clapping were heard from the audience.

"Will you accept these into the corporation?" shouted the man whose tone had become a kind of pleading as if all of sudden he was hugely in favour of the idea.

The applause and cheering grew.

"I can't hear you," shouted the man in yellow.

The noise increased.

"Louder!"

The audience erupted as one in cheering, whooping and hollering every bit as loud as it had been during the booing and cussing just a few minutes prior. The yellow man allowed this to continue before raising his hand for silence one last time.

"Very well. You have convinced me. I will need two volunteers to consummate the ceremony."

A number of hands went up from the crowd and the man in yellow selected two who skipped up the stage enthusiastically and stood directly behind JJ and Krusty, so close that JJ could feel the man's breath on his neck.

"What's the consummation?" JJ asked him.

"You're about to find out, sweetheart," grinned the man.

"And I'll need eight enforcers," announced the man in yellow.

Again, many hands went up and the man chose the allotted number.

"Dude, what does he need enforcers for?" said Krusty who was even starting to sound a little worried.

The eight volunteers, all large men, ascended to the stage and took up a position so that they formed a square around JJ and another around Krusty.

"Disrobe them," commanded the man in yellow.

From behind him, JJ felt the belt around his pink bathrobe be untied and then the robe itself pulled down violently from his shoulders forcing his arms downwards. In perfect unison, as if they had practiced the manoeuvre before, two of the enforcers grabbed an arm each and twisted in such a way as to force JJ to the ground whereupon the other two fell on his feet and pulled back so that before he knew what had happened he was lying on his back with arms pulled back to the side and above his head. He looked across to see that the same had happened to Krusty with the exception that he had managed to pry one foot loose and was flailing his leg about like a wild horse.

"Fuck off, bro!" he shouted as the man finally got the foot under control and thrust an elbow downwards into Krusty's thigh as punishment.

The crowd began a chant that started quietly and then got progressively louder – "Hail Macbeth. Slay Duncan. Hail Macbeth. Slay Duncan" – it rang out over and over.

From his position on the ground looking up at the ceiling, JJ saw the man tasked with consummating the ceremony take a step forward such that his feet were about level with JJ's chest one foot on either side of his body as he faced towards JJ's feet. From this unusual angle, JJ struggled to make out what the man was doing. Was he scratching his stomach? Or tucking his shirt in? It wasn't until JJ caught sight of the tail end of the man's belt that he realised the man had undone the belt and was in the process of undoing the fly on his jeans and, just as the true horror of the situation became apparent to JJ, he saw - *it* - and no sooner had he seen - *it* - than he saw a stream of light yellow fluid coming out of *it* glimmering off the lights of the room and twinkling down onto JJ's bare midriff. It wasn't so much the sensation on his skin as the knowledge of what was going on that that caused JJ to begin writhing around like a cut snake.

"Fuck off," he shouted but he could barely even hear his own voice above the chanting "Hail Macbeth. Slay Duncan."

"Hey, stop squirming. You're getting piss everywhere," shouted the man who was holding his left arm.

"I'm getting piss everywhere!?" cried JJ hysterically as he looked over to see that two extra men had run over to help keep Krusty pinned to the floor while the same thing was happening to him.

That made a total of six men who looked like they were trying to wrestle a crocodile and only just winning.

The whole thing seemed to go on far longer than the physiology of the human bladder should have allowed, but finally the flow of yellow fluid stopped and the consummators zipped up their pants, did up their belts and took a step back. The four, or in the case of Krusty, six, enforcers pulled JJ and Krusty to their feet and presented them to the crowd who broke into wild cheering and clapping like it was the end of the last song at a rock concert. The cheering went on for some time until the man in yellow, the colour of which now made more sense to JJ, once again beckoned for quiet at which point JJ and Krusty were turned around and led over to stand in front of Macbeth who had sat there during the whole ritual with a stern and uncompromising look on her face like the statue of an ancient goddess. She gazed upon them for a few seconds with this look before suddenly bursting out in laughter. She stood and clapped her hands together.

"This always cracks me up," she giggled. "Alright, the ceremony is consummated. Go and hose them down."

The enforcers dragged JJ and Krusty back to the meat locker from which they had come. Snake and Ciara were already there with hoses in hand. The men pushed them to the middle of the room and a burst of cold water hit them like a slap in the face. After a thorough drenching, they were thrown a towel each.

"Dude, what the fuck was that?" said Krusty once he had recovered from the shock.

"Welcome to the Macbeth Corporation," grinned Snake. "A baptism of fire, isn't it."

"Pretty sure that wasn't holy water," said JJ ruefully.

"Well, if you two stop whining and get yourselves dry we'll take you out for some proper holy water."

"What's that?"

"The final stage of the initiation," said Ciara.

"What, you're gonna make us drink piss now?"

"Yeah, but not that kind of piss."

"It involves a lot of vodka."

"You did well," smiled Ciara as she took the towel from Krusty and handed him his t-shirt. "I've never seen six men needed to hold somebody down before. You must be *really* strong."

It might have been the tone of her voice, it might have been her lascivious smile or the fact that she was running her hand down his bare chest, but Krusty's anger evaporated and before long both he and JJ were dressed and walking back to the main room to meet their new comrades and drink a toast to the newest associates of the Macbeth Corporation.

Chapter 2

"Dude, I want a fuckin' lawyer," yelled Krusty as the cop turned the key on the jail cell door and guffawed as he walked back towards the front door.

"Nearest lawyer's two hundred k's away, princess. You might be waiting a while."

"Then I want a phone call," shouted Krusty but the cop was now out of sight and didn't respond.

It was ten days since JJ and Krusty had been initiated into the Macbeth Corporation, nine days since they had begun trading in cash and one minute since they'd been thrown in jail.

The day after their initiation, Snake took them through the rather mundane logistics of laundering financial transactions using the system that was already in extensive use within the Macbeth Corporation. They were set up with a bank account to which customers would make electronic transfers. JJ or Krusty would then make cash withdrawals from the same account minus the Macbeth handling fee of five percent. They were then free to charge whatever fee they wanted on top and that would constitute their profit from the transaction. It was an incredibly simple system that also proved to be incredibly popular. No sooner had they arrived back in Tittybong than the money started rolling in. A far greater proportion of Tittybong's residents were reliant on money from the city than anybody knew. Within days, half the town came knocking on JJ's door asking for cash. That was the good part.

The bad part was that Tittybong was a small town and word about the new operation eventually got to the police which saw Constable Dawkins and Sergeant Smith come knocking on JJ's door that morning. JJ's insistence that it wasn't legal to arrest somebody without stating the specific crime they were charged with got a chuckle from the two policemen. His subsequent shrieking that Smith and Dawkins were "imbeciles" who didn't understand that the Global Council was about to remove all cash from circulation and that within days the police themselves wouldn't be able to collect their wages got an outright laugh.

"We got ourselves a couple of conspiracy theorists here, Smith," laughed Dawkins as he snapped the cuffs around JJ's wrists and pushed him outside to the waiting police van.

Several onlookers, who had to come to JJ's house to collect their cash, also protested to the police but all in vain. The Tittybong police were not known for their empathy or intelligence either of which might have led them to understand exactly how close they were to being lynched by a group of people for whom not being able to get their hands on the money which was owing to them was not simply a disappointment on a Thursday morning but a matter of existential importance especially because word had got around that the cash ban would become all-encompassing in just a few days' time. None of this mattered to Smith and Dawkins who were delighted to be able to arrest somebody for once, an opportunity that came along very seldom in the sleepy backwater that was Tittybong. And so JJ and Krusty had become the only inmates of the Tittybong prison which was a small bluestone building set back behind the police station on Park Street.

Krusty kicked the cell door and made his way back to where JJ was sitting.

"This is bullshit, bro. These dipshits couldn't even get organised enough to charge us with an actual crime."

JJ said nothing and Krusty looked over to see him staring absently at his shoes.

"What's the matter with you? Oi!"

Krusty gave JJ a whack on the arm which roused him from his daydream.

"What?" he asked without looking up.

"This is bullshit, right?"

"Sure is."

"Well, what are we gonna do about it?"

"There's not much we can do. Who's gonna stick up for us here? Certainly not the mayor or anybody in a position of authority and it'll take days to get a lawyer out here even if they do give us one."

"Bastards."

"Anyway, that's not the main problem. The main problem is that in three days the cash supply is gonna dry up and then what happens to Tittybong? None of these idiots even knows what's coming."

"Maybe they'll let us out when they realise we were right?"

"Or when they want some cash for themselves since we'll be the only one who'll have any."

"Dude, they're probably stealing it all from your house right now."

"Yeah. And if it's not the cops stealing it, it'll be somebody else."

There was loud crack from the front of the building and JJ and Krusty heard footsteps approaching which portended the re-appearance of Sergeant Smith who walked over and put the key into the lock of the cell door.

"Decided to do the right thing and give us our phone call, have you, bro?" asked Krusty.

"You don't need a phone call, Mr Crowley. You've made bail," announced the officer as he swung open the door.

"What? Who got us bail?" asked JJ.

"Why don't you come outside and see? He's waiting for you."

"No way, bro. This sounds like a trick."

"There's no trick. Now hurry the hell up before I change my mind."

JJ gave Krusty a whack and they jumped up and hurried out of the cell and down the short corridor that led to the front door where the glare of the midday sun stung their eyes preventing for a few moments the recognition that the figure straight ahead was none other than Snake dressed in his usual outfit of motorcycle leathers.

"Hello, gentleman. Your legal team has arrived," he said with a faux-theatrical flourish.

"Snake?" mumbled JJ. "How did you get here so quick?"

"We'll talk about that in a minute, Mr JJ. Thank you, Smitty."

Snake slapped Sergeant Smith on the shoulder as he walked past him and into the police station through the back door.

"Alright, gents. Why don't we take a walk. We've got some things to discuss."

Snake led them down the side of the police station to a gate near the back which opened into the town park. Just ahead was a wooden table under a pergola near the barbecue where he gestured for them to sit.

"So, is getting bailed out of jail one of the perks offered by membership of the Macbeth Corporation?" asked JJ sliding his leg over the wooden bench seat.

"The Corporation always takes care of its own, Mr JJ."

"You came all the way out here to bail us out?"

"Not exactly. I came out to pay you a visit and when I found your house empty I made some enquiries. Fortunately, we were expecting some trouble with the police so this gave me an excuse to organise things with our friends in the force sooner rather than later."

"You made them a deal too good to refuse?"

"Something like that. Anyway, that's all taken care of now so we can discuss the thing that I really came to Tittybong to talk to you about. I have a proposition for you. Or, rather, the Corporation does."

"Are you making us a deal too good to refuse too?"

"I am just a messenger, my friend. The Corporation needs your help. If memory serves me correctly, you both heard the end of our leader's speech just before your initiation ceremony. Do you remember what she said?"

"Not really, bro. Although, I think my memory might have been scarred by getting pissed on," said Krusty.

"You still bitter about that, K-man?"

"She said something about vanquishing the globalist scum," said JJ. "Sticking a dagger into their hearts."

"Very good, Mr JJ. You've got a good memory. Needless to say, our leader is not a fan of the Global Council. Now, an opportunity has arisen for us to take real action against our enemies. Our sources inside the government have told us that there is to be a congress of the Global Council that will take place in Sydney in just a few days' time. The announcement has been kept secret until the last minute for security purposes. The congress coincides with the new measures such as the cash ban which are coming into place. You probably don't know this, but there will be cash bans and movement restrictions across the globe, at least in the countries that are under control of the Global Council. The congress will announce the implementation of these and other measures."

"What's that got to do with us, bro?" asked Krusty.

"Patience, K-man. I'm getting to that. Now, we are informed that all members of the Global Council will be present in Sydney for the congress including the leader, Kurt von Todhammerstein. Todhammerstein will be giving a speech on the final day of the congress that will be televised globally. He will announce that the new measures are the beginning of a new era in global governance. He wants it to be a victory speech. Given this is all going to take place in our backyard, we have a unique opportunity to fight our enemy on our own turf."

"You're gonna assassinate Todhammerstein?" said JJ.

"Not exactly. Assassinating him out in the open is not the best move in the circumstances. Firstly, such a mission would be dangerous and unlikely to succeed. Todhammerstein is extremely paranoid and is surrounded by an armed guard of crack security personnel at all times. Secondly, we could expect retaliation from the globalist forces directly and that is not in our interests."

"So, what's the plan then?" asked JJ who was struggling to see how this could have anything to do with him or Krusty.

"We're going to have him catch a cold," said Snake as if this statement made perfect sense.

He looked eagerly at JJ and Krusty expecting them to ascertain the genius of the design but the blank stares he received in return indicated more information was required.

"Right. You two don't know anything about Todhammerstein, do you."

Snake let out a long sigh as if contemplating a large amount of work that was going to be required of him.

"Look, long story short, Todhammerstein is a germaphobe."

"What's a germaphobe?" asked Krusty.

"It's a person who's afraid of germs," said Snake impatiently. "Don't interrupt and I'll explain. Todhammerstein is a germaphobe and so are the rest of the Global Council. Not only are they germaphobes, they believe that with advances in science and technology humans will be able to live forever. This is one of the core elements of the philosophy of the Global Council and Todhammerstein owes his position as President largely to the political power he has won through promising a life free of disease leading to the promise of eternal life. This has won him power not only among the Global Council but also its followers in the governments of the various countries that are now under the rule of the Council. It is this ideology that needs to be killed. We believe having Todhammerstein catch a cold would achieve that goal by removing the veneer of invincibility that surrounds him."

JJ's head was swimming from all the information.

"Ok. But I still don't see what this has to do with us," he said.

"Now that you know the background, let me outline the plan and how you fit into it. Alongside being a germaphobe, Todhammerstein is also a fanatical vegan. As part of the congress he has announced a competition aimed at finding the best kale growers in the world."

"What the fuck is kale, bro?"

Snake again sighed at being interrupted.

"It's a vegetable of the brassica family."

"What the fuck is a brassica?"

"It doesn't matter. Just let me finish. There will be a kale growing competition but, and this is where you two come into the picture, the competition is to see who can grow the best kale using hydroponics. For some reason hydroponics are all the rage among the Global Council techno-nerds at the moment. Now, correct me if I'm wrong, but Krusty here uses hydroponics to grow his weed, which is universally recognised as the highest quality weed on the market I might add."

"Yeah, I use hydroponics. But I grow weed, bro, not vegetables."

"If you can grow weed, you can grow kale. The point is this, the kale growing competition is Todhammerstein's pet project. He will personally award the winners of the competition. That gives us a rare opportunity to bypass his personal guard and get in the same room with him. Understand?"

"Not really, bro."

"Let me spell it out for you. We want you to enter the kale growing competition. Once inside, you will infect Todhammerstein with a cold virus. Because the whole thing happens invisibly, nobody will be able to trace the cause back to us. As Todhammerstein's power is predicated on conquering disease, him catching a cold will cause the failure of the ideology itself especially if he is forced to get up and address the entire world at the congress while having the flu."

JJ sat there dumbstruck before Krusty put both their thoughts into words.

"Dude, that's the dumbest fucking plan I've ever heard and I've heard some pretty dumb plans in my time."

"That's your opinion and you're welcome to it," said Snake gruffly.

"The chances of this working are one in a million," said JJ.

"I admit this is not a foolproof plan. Rest assured it is one of many the Corporation will be undertaking. In any case, we think the chances of success make it worth the time and effort. Now, the question you should ask is what's in it for you. Let me assure you there will be a significant financial reward for taking this mission and it will be doubled if you complete the mission successfully. The money you are earning here in lovely Tittybong is chicken feed compared to what you will receive by accepting. If you successfully complete this mission you can buy your own house and live in Kirribilli if you want. And if I may add a personal incentive, Mr JJ here has pointed out that his ex-girlfriend's father is involved with the Global Council. Wouldn't you like to take some revenge, Mr JJ?"

JJ looked at Snake's slippery smile and instantly regretted using him to get the photos of Amber. The truth was he'd never met Amber's father and they'd never talked about politics. JJ had no idea what her father even did, even though he was technically the Prime Minister of Australia. He certainly had no desire for revenge against a man he barely knew.

"How could we even enter the competition?" said JJ trying to find fault with the plan rather than object to it outright. "Surely, they wouldn't accept a couple of country bumpkins with no credentials."

"We will get you in. There is a team travelling up from Melbourne to take part in the contest. They will have an unfortunate car accident on the way and you will take their places and arrive at the North Shore pretending to be them."

"Great. So apart from anything else, we have to go undercover as well. What happens if we get busted?"

"We will do our best to help you if that happens. As I say, the Corporation always takes care of its own."

"But we'll be in the lion's den."

"There's an element of danger in the mission, I will admit."

"No shit, bro. And we're the ones who will cop the fallout if the whole thing goes tits up."

"You said this was a proposal and not a command, right? What happens if we say no?" asked JJ.

"Nothing happens, Mr JJ. The Corporation does not like to coerce its members into things they do not want to do. If you decide the mission is not for you, you will be free to stay here in Tittybong and run our financial operations as you have been doing for the last week. To great success, I hear. How much have you made? A few hundred bucks?"

"Will we be able to continue our financial operations here?" asked JJ.

"Yeah, bro, what about the cops?" added Krusty.

"I told you, I've taken care of them. In just three days' time, the police here will be on the Macbeth payroll."

"Why?"

"Because in three days they will no longer be earning a salary from the government."

"So, Macbeth now owns the cops?"

"It's all part of the plan, gentlemen. You heard Macbeth's speech. The Corporation will be taking over where the Global Council retreats. We expect towns like Tittybong to become pillars of the resistance moving forward."

"So, you'll own the money supply and the cops."

"Exactly. And not just in Tittybong. You've joined the Corporation at a very exciting time. It's not just the future of Tittybong that is up for grabs but the fate of the whole nation. If we manage to remove the globalist scourge from our shores we will form a government of our own that will once again reunify the country."

"With Macbeth as the Queen?" asked JJ.

"Sounds like a dictatorship to me, bro."

"Yeah, and what about the existing Australian government?" asked JJ.

"Hah, they'll be a pushover," cackled Snake. "With Todhammerstein out of the way, we'll remove them by force."

JJ suddenly realised the extent of the situation and the role within in it that he and Krusty had stumbled into. It was fun to do business with the mob while still retaining a degree of autonomy and control over your destiny. But they were now card carrying members of an organisation that was apparently about to organise a coup against not just the globalist government but the rightful, if subservient, Australian government. They were now actively involved in an insurrection that aimed to overthrow the national parliament and put in its place a dictator who happened to be a twelve year old girl. The only upside was that the plan for taking out Todhammerstein seemed to have been concocted by a twelve year old and was so ridiculous that it could never work.

"Well, I assume from the lack of any more questions that you've both understood the situation. That was a lot of information to take in. Why don't I give you a bit of time to think it over," said Snake getting up from the table. "I'll give you until the end of the day to make your decision. If you haven't called me by 9 o'clock, I'll assume you're out."

"Ok, thanks," said JJ absently.

"Oh, and by the way, if you say yes," said Snake over his shoulder as he walked away, "you'll need to be in Sydney by midday tomorrow. And don't forget, if you accept, we'll make you richer than you ever thought possible."

With that he swung around disappeared around the corner that led back to the road. Krusty gave a dismissive snort, pulled out a bag of weed and began rolling a joint.

"I dunno what these guys are smoking, dude. But that's the dumbest shit I've ever heard. We're gonna take down a global empire by making somebody catch a cold. I thought Macbeth was supposed to be a smart operator."

"Yeah, it doesn't make any sense to me either," said JJ getting up off the wooden bench and pacing around the barbecue area.

He stopped in his tracks as if he'd had a revelation.

"What if they're lying. Yeah, that's gotta be it. They're trying to set us up."

"Whaddya mean?" said Krusty lighting his joint.

"Of course. It has to be that. They don't really need us to win the competition so why else would they need us? To be the fall guys. They're gonna assassinate Todhammerstein and then pin it on us."

"Makes sense. But why such a ridiculous story? What's all this bullshit about getting Todhammerstein to catch a cold."

"I dunno. Maybe they want to poison him and the cold thing is just a cover story. Man, they must really think we're a couple of idiots."

"Country bumpkins, bro."

"Well, I guess that settles it. We'll tell Snake we're not gonna do it."

"Too easy, dude. We'll just have to sit back here and count our money. Do you know how much profit we made in the last week?"

"A thousand bucks."

"A thousand bucks, bro. And now the whole thing is totally legit and the cops are off our back and everything."

"If by the *legit* you mean run and organised by the most notorious mob boss in the country who just happens to be a twelve year old girl who wants to overthrow the government."

"Hey, you can't have everything. Anyway, Macbeth doesn't seem that bad to me. She's the only one doing anything for Tittybong."

"She's a megalomaniac running a criminal organisation."

"How's that different to any other politician?"

"Maybe so. But once upon a time we were at least able to choose the best megalomaniac. Once Macbeth is in power, she'll have full control of everything."

"What? You care about politics now?"

"It's a pretty good time to start caring about politics, don't you think?"

"Nope. There's nothing much we can do about it, is there?"

"I guess not," said JJ sitting back down on the wooden bench just as Krusty's phone began to ring.

"Hey, bro," said Krusty answering the call. "What? Oh, shit. Yeah, no worries, dude. We'll be right there."

Krusty hung up the phone and took one last, hurried puff on his joint before putting it out on the table.

"Dude, we gotta get back to the house. Sammy says there's a shitload of people hanging around waiting to get cash and they're talking about kicking the door down."

"Ok. Can you take care of it, man? I need some time to think."

"Alright, bro. Don't let your brains fall out, though."

"Huh?"

"Don't think too hard," said Krusty over his shoulder as he rushed out of the park in the direction their house.

JJ watched him go then let out a long sigh and lay down on the wooden bench looking up to the blue, cloudless sky through the leaves of a nearby gum tree whose branches stretched out high above his head. To say that it had been a tumultuous period in his life would have been an understatement. In the space of a month he had lost his girl and then potentially his livelihood. He had joined the mob, started earning money in amounts he could never have dreamed of and then got thrown in jail. And now there was this ridiculous offer to help topple the world government coming on the back of the equally ridiculous ceremony at Macbeth's headquarters just over a week earlier.

The chant of "Hail Macbeth, Slay Duncan" popped into his head as he thought back to the night of the initiation. The initiation itself came so unexpectedly and was over so quickly that he remembered it in exactly that same way you might remember a bad nightmare. It was what happened afterwards that had made him regret becoming a member of the Corporation. Krusty had disappeared with Ciara almost immediately leaving JJ alone in the bar. Although nowhere near as uncomfortable as he'd been in the pink dressing gown, he still felt out of place dressed in his usual jeans and white t-shirt combination. The discomfort didn't improve when, while trying to make small talk with a couple of the black leather clad heavily-tattooed dudes at the bar he'd made some silly crack about never believing that Macbeth was a twelve year old girl if he hadn't seen it with his own eyes. He'd quickly found himself pinned back against the bar with threats of having his lights punched out. Fortunately, Snake was within hearing distance and had rushed over to save his bacon. A similar pattern repeated itself over the course of the evening, although he'd learned to be extra discreet about his wording. Whenever the subject of

Macbeth came up a quasi-religious atmosphere took hold and, even though almost everybody in the room was an amicable and easy going person to talk with on any other subject, the name of Macbeth seemed to function like a switch that turned them into snarling fanatics.

JJ figured it was best to avoid the subject. In fact, he set out to do as little talking as possible and concentrated instead of listening. The hot topic of conversation was a raft of new measures that Macbeth had laid out prior to JJ's initiation ceremony. These included the announcement that Macbeth intended to take over the supply of cash once the government moved entirely to digital transactions. This held not just for the country towns but also for the black market operations in the city. With the closing of the city walls, Macbeth would operate a transportation service at a fee to smuggle people in and out of the cities. The announcement of a banking service to turn electronic transactions into cash also came up in conversation and JJ got himself into trouble a second time by suggesting that the idea was his. Fortunately, he was just written off as a braggart. The overall impression JJ got was of an organisation that was superficially casual and informal and yet highly directed, focused and militant. People talked openly of insurrection and overthrowing the globalists but, more troublingly, about discarding the Australian government and installing Macbeth in its place. At the time, JJ took it about as seriously as a pink bathrobe but after hearing Snake's offer he now realised they were deadly serious. Although the business about having Todhammerstein catch a cold was clearly made up, he was in no doubt that they wanted to take him out. The only question was how and why they wanted him and Krusty.

Two thoughts battled for primacy in JJ's mind. First, was what Snake would do if they declined the offer. JJ had already been surprised by some of the unconventional methods of the Corporation and he couldn't shake the feeling that the ostensibly voluntary nature of the proposition was all a façade and that he and Krusty were expected to say yes or face ramifications. What those ramifications were was anybody's guess but the simple reality was that even if it was something simple like getting kicked out of the Corporation, how would they survive in the new world where, at least for the short term, Macbeth was going to be in control of Tittybong owning not just the money supply but the cops. As uncomfortable as the whole thing made him, it was still better to be on the inside for now.

This led to the second thought that was rattling around in his mind which was what the world would look like if Macbeth succeeded. Those fanatics inside the Corporation would be running the country. But, more importantly, Macbeth would be sitting at the top of it all and that was the one big unknown because he had no idea what she actually stood for. What could a twelve year old girl stand for anyway? Whatever it was, it didn't seem to be logic and reason. The spell she cast over a room full of grown adults who in any other area of their life would have seemed perfectly normal, barring the neck tattoos and nose rings, made JJ very uneasy. He quite liked the old Tittybong. It was in many respects dysfunctional but the dysfunction gave you room to move. It gave you freedom to try things like selling second hand goods. The Macbeth Corporation seemed highly functional but that was half the problem. They were just as efficient at making people disappear without a trace as organising financial transactions. They would no doubt be extremely competent at stifling dissent and putting any kind of opposition out of action. Whatever sort of state it would be under Macbeth, it would be a one party state. One corporation to rule them all. And he and Krusty had unwittingly become pawns in the machine.

All of this worked to create a great pressure on him. He felt the iron grip of the "voluntary" offer closing in just like the iron grip that Macbeth would exercise on every facet of life in Tittybong. Loyalty to the Corporation or else. That was what was on offer. And yet he had no notion of any way out of the situation. He and Krusty could do a runner but where would they run to?

After an hour or so running these ideas through his mind, JJ got up and made his way back to his and Krusty's house on the outskirts of town. He instantly regretted it. To say the house was heaving was an understatement. It seemed that half the town was hanging around trying to get their hands on some cash. He wasn't ready to face that scene and so he snuck in through the back and slinked into his bedroom and closed the door. As he flopped himself down on the bed he realised another problem with the current situation which was that he and Krusty were going to be very high profile members of the Macbeth Corporation in Tittybong. This was very different from selling second hand electronic goods where the origin of the goods was unknown both to JJ and to the customer and JJ could, in theory, have found another supplier if he needed to. He'd had a level of independence and autonomy. Now he had neither and as the suppliers of the town's money he was a very visible and very crucial representative of the Macbeth Corporation and its impending takeover of Tittybong.

Once again he was psychically swamped by a feeling of being stuck in a vice with no way out. He lifted himself off the bed as if a change of bodily position might give him a new perspective and caught sight of a manila folder on the desk by the window. He walked over and flipped open the cover to reveal the photo of Amber as seen through her bedroom window. He flicked through the other photos as he had already done a hundred times before and felt the slight heartache that came from running his eyes over Amber's pretty face. He stopped his perusal at one of the photos in the middle of the stack. It was one of Amber on her front doorstep kissing her father goodbye. JJ hadn't paid this one much attention before but now it took on a new significance. He remembered Snake's quip about how the surveillance of Amber was made easy by the fact that the Corporation already had a man watching her father. Then he remembered how Snake had raised the subject of Amber's father as a way to get JJ to take the mission. Something clicked in his mind and he realised the plan to take out the Australian government must have been in place for some time. It was no idle threat. They could just as easily swap the photographer that was surveilling Johansson with a sniper. That's why Macbeth had somebody watching Amber's father, he *was* the Australian government. Although, the parliament of Australia hadn't convened in years, Florian Johansson was still nominally the Prime Minister. What this meant was that Amber was in the firing line, literally and figuratively. What happened if Macbeth's hitmen came for her father and she happened to be home at the time? He didn't even want to think about it.

And then a final and chilling possibility entered his mind: what if the only reason Snake wanted him for the mission was because of his connection to Amber's father? That would make sense. It seemed like the only thing that could make sense. Why else would he come all the way to Tittybong to get a couple of, in his own words, *hillbillies* for such an important mission? Surely they could find somebody better from within the Corporation itself; somebody with more experience who knew how to go undercover. And if they just needed a couple of patsies, then there must have been others who were easier to find in Sydney. But Snake knew about JJ's connection with Amber and her father.

A thousand thoughts rushed through JJ's mind but there was one thought uppermost and it was with that thought that he rushed out of the bedroom and into the lounge where

Krusty was seated on the couch surrounded by about a half dozen people.

"There you are, dude," said Krusty to JJ as he walked in. "About time, I could use a little help here."

"I need to talk to you," said JJ. "In private."

"Let's do it later, bro. We've got customers."

Krusty gestured to the people standing in front of him. They were each holding a small slip of paper which contained their bank account details and the amount they were wanting to transfer which Krusty was processing through a laptop computer sitting on the coffee table before him.

"Excuse me, folks," said JJ to the people. "This will only take a few minutes."

He grabbed hold the sleeve of Krusty's t-shirt and pulled him towards the storage room at the front of the house closing the door behind them.

"Dude, what the fuck. Can't you see we're busy?"

"We need to take the mission?"

"What mission?"

"Snake's mission. We need to go to Sydney and take part in this kale growing competition."

"Are you stoned, bro?"

"No, I'm not stoned. Listen, I know why Snake wants us."

"Why?"

"Because I know Amber and therefore I have a connection to Amber's father who they are going to take out."

"Oh, man. Not the Amber thing again. I thought you were over that shit, dude."

"Think about it. Why else would Macbeth want us, a couple of nobodies from the bush, to do a mission we have no training or experience for? Why would they want to use a couple of new members when they must have far more reliable and trustworthy people they could use? None of it makes sense. But we know they want to take out the government and Amber's father will be the first one the list."

"Ok. Even if that were true, that's be a pretty fucking good reason *not* to go. Or do you actually want to help them take out Amber's father?"

"Of course I don't. I want to warn Amber and her father. But we can only do that from the inside. That's why we need to take the mission."

"This just sounds to me like an excuse to try and see Amber again. You wanna show up like 007 going undercover and she'll throw herself at you like a Bond girl."

"No, I don't."

"Look, bro. If you wanna take the mission, fine. Do that. You can go and just leave me here."

"I need you. You're the horticulture expert. I don't know how to work a hydroponics system."

"Neither do I."

"Bullshit, you don't. You're the grower of Krusty's Special; the best-selling brand of weed in Sydney."

Krusty let out a long sigh.

"Look, dude, I have a confession to make. But you have to promise not to say anything after I tell you."

"Ok, I promise."

"I'm serious, bro. My entire reputation would be undermined by what I'm about to tell you."

"Yeah, I get it. I won't say anything."

"I don't grow the weed."

"What weed?"

"Krusty's special. I don't grow it. I buy it from someone else. I'm just the salesman. I've never used a hydroponics thingo in my life."

"I thought you said you grew it in a place out in the bush."

"Well, technically, it does get grown in a place in the bush. Just not by me."

"Then who grows it?"

"Remember Svenson from high school?"

"The Norwegian guy?"

"Yeah. He grows it. He's the real hydroponics expert."

JJ took some time to digest this bit of news.

"Man, I can't believe you've been lying all these years."

"Sorry, bro. But that's how it is. So, we can't do the mission, I'm afraid."

"What about Svenson?"

"What about him?"

"We can ask him to do the mission."

"Nah, bro. Trust me. He's not gonna be into that. He's a total loner. He comes into town twice a year. That's why he lives off grid in the bush."

"So what? We have to ask. It sounds like he's our only chance. I'll help you finish off serving these people then we'll go and see him."

"Svenson doesn't like surprises, bro."

"I don't care. C'mon, let's get this done and then take a ride out bush."

***

It was about an hour's ride due east from Tittybong twisting up the mountains that formed the great dividing range to get to Svenson's off grid ranch. The road became progressively less hospitable until they turned off on what was little more than a dirt track and rounded a bend to see a peculiar conglomeration of dark green trees forming the border of a large block that stood out from the surrounding eucalyptus-dominated forest by the density of the foliage. JJ leaned gently into his motorbike and followed Krusty down the driveway where they parked and removed their riding gear.

"Now just remember, bro, Svenson is a little bit weird. Actually, he's a lot weird. So, don't be surprised if he says some things that don't make much sense."

"He sounds like just what we need, given that nothing has made sense for the last two weeks."

"Whaddya mean *we*?"

"What? You're not gonna come with us?"

"Nah, bro. I'm happy to hang back here. Somebody's gotta hold the fort."

"You know what will happen if you do that?"

"What?"

"Snake will know that you're not the real grower of Krusty's Special."

"How would he know that?"

"I'll have to tell him?"

"Why?"

"So, he knows that Svenson is legit. Otherwise, he could be just any random dude I pulled in for the mission."

"Just make up some bullshit about how he's also a hydroponics wizard."

"What if they ask for proof. We'll have to give them some of Krusty's Special which is really Svenson's Special and then they'll figure it out for themselves."

"Whatever, dude. Let's go and talk to Svenson first. Pretty sure he's gonna tell you stick your mission where the sun don't shine anyway."

Krusty opened the gate at the side of the house and led JJ through the small backyard area towards a huge building that was more like an industrial factory than a backyard shed. They transitioned from the cool, dry mountain air outside straight into what felt more like a tropical jungle. The humidity hit JJ in the face like a wet rag and beads of moisture instantly began running down his face. Inside the factory it was a wall of green with row after perfectly ordered row of stands about a metre or so wide holding up vessels through which hoses snaked. There was a muffled sound of running water bubbling through the building and countless dope plants each about a metre tall grew up out of the containers.

"Svenson!" shouted Krusty but there was no response.

"He's probably down the back."

Krusty beckoned for JJ to follow him and they walked down one of the aisles. JJ noted the incredible cleanliness and orderliness of the place. Not a spot of dirt could be seen on the floor and even the dope plants themselves seemed to be identical in height and shape as if each was a carbon copy of the last. Finally, they got to the end of the aisle where there was a short clearing leading to a large office with glass windows through which a tall, blonde man could be seen crouched over a computer with a large set of headphones over his ears. As they approached the doorway, JJ could hear the distinctive screech of black metal emanating from the headphones like a satanic chipmunk. Krusty knocked on the door but that was of little use so he took a step into the office and began waving his arms over his head to capture Svenson's attention. This went on for several seconds with the arm waving growing more and more frantic until it became clear that Svenson was perfectly well aware of their presence and was simply finishing off whatever he was doing on the computer. He pressed a few buttons which brought the screeching in the headphones to a stop then looked up at them with an expression that signalled no particular emotion at their appearance before him.

"You're three days early," he said flatly.

"What? Yeah, nah, bro. We're not here to collect weed. We're here about another thing. We, umm, we need your, well, JJ was gonna tell you anyway. This is JJ. JJ, this is Svenson."

"Hey, man," said JJ giving a little wave to which Svenson gave no response.

After an awkward silence, JJ figured this was an invitation for him to proceed to the business at hand.

"So, ummm, we need your help, man, because you're the hydroponics expert around here and there's a competition happening in Sydney to see who can grow the best kale using hydroponics methods. The competition is run by the Global Council who we're trying to overthrow but we need to win the competition to get near enough to the leader of the Council to take him out cos he's gonna be the judge of the competition. And, umm, we need to get right up close with him because we're gonna make him catch a cold. That's, err, how we're gonna do it. Right? Does that make sense?" said JJ who became painfully aware of the absurdity of what he was saying as he was saying it.

Svenson still gave no response so JJ figured he would try another tack.

"Look, long story short, dude, we need you to come to Sydney with us and win a kale growing competition."

"I told you not to come here stoned," said Svenson looking at Krusty with disapproval.

"We're not stoned, bro. This is legit," said Krusty. "I know it sounds weird but it's legit. There is a kale growing competition and we want to win it."

"Cabbage? You want me to help you grow cabbage?"

"Nah, dude. Kale."

"Kale is cabbage," snapped Svenson who was finally showing some sign of emotion although not the emotion JJ was hoping for.

"Ok. We need you to help us grow cabbage then."

"Any moron can grow cabbage. Using hydroponics to grow cabbage is like using a sledgehammer to squash an ant."

"It's not our idea," said JJ. "That's what the Global Council want to do."

"Then they are imbeciles."

"But that's good, right. That means it will be easy to win the competition."

"Do you know the difference between growing cabbage and growing weed?" asked Svenson who walked out from behind the desk and gestured out the window to the factory floor.

"It's like the difference between Beethoven and some shitty pop song. It's like holding a concert at the Albert Hall featuring Mozart only he spends three hours playing Baa Baa Black Sheep and Mary Had a Little Lamb. It's an affront to one's intelligence. An insult to even contemplate the matter."

"Ok, man. We get it. It's not a good idea. But winning the competition is just the first part of the plan. The point of winning the competition is so that we can get into close contact with the Global Council and take them down from within. Have you heard about the new cash bans or the moves to shut off the cities? That's why we're doing this. It's not really about the competition."

"And?" shrugged Svenson.

"You can be an integral part of putting a stop to all that."

"I don't care about politics," said Svenson returning back behind his desk and taking a seat.

"You need cash, don't you? The Global Council is going to ban cash. Won't that be a problem for you?"

"Not really. The cool thing about weed is that almost everybody is happy to trade it for something of value. Just last week I bartered a few ounces for a side of beef."

"Ok, but what about Macbeth. Don't you know that if the Global Council puts its plan into action then Macbeth will be taking over the money supply and the governance of this whole area?"

"Macbeth is the main customer for my product."

"Well, what about an adventure? Wouldn't you like a change of scenery? A trip to Sydney fully paid?"

"Sydney? A den of iniquity. A vile pit of despair and greed where every vice finds a home and every virtue is smothered by the blanket of human vanity."

"A reward? Big wads of cash that you can use to buy the latest hydroponics gear or improve your black metal music collection," said JJ who was fast coming to the end of the list of things he had devised to convince Svenson to help.

"Crass materialism does not impress me."

JJ sighed.

"Well, that's it then. We're fucked. We're either going to be governed by Todhammerstein or by Macbeth. Either way, this country is in deep trouble."

JJ's shoulders slumped as he turned around and looked out the window onto the rows and rows of hydroponics equipment and plants.

After a few seconds, Svenson broke the silence.

"What do you mean, *Todhammerstein*?"

"What?" said JJ turning around from the window.

"You said, Australia would be governed by *Todhammerstein*?"

"Yep. Sure did."

"Kurt Wilhelm Friedrich Gustav Johann von Todhammerstein?"

"Uhh, I think so. I dunno about his middle names. I just know him as Kurt von Todhammerstein. He's the leader of the Global Council."

Svenson turned to his computer and reeled off a flurry of keystrokes.

"Muthafucker!" he shouted slamming his fist into the desk causing both JJ and Krusty to take an instinctive step back.

"Is everything ok, bro?" asked Krusty cautiously.

"Kurt Wilhelm Friedrich Gustav Johann von Todhammerstein is the second cousin once removed of the Archduke of Lower Saxony's grandfather, sworn nemesis of Olaf of Oslo the third."

"Can you repeat that in English, bro."

"Olaf of Oslo was the illegitimate son of my great great grandfather banished from the kingdom to deprive him of his rightful place on the throne. Our family has sought in vain for vengeance for this grievous crime ever since. What does Todhammerstein have to do with your kale competition?"

"He's the judge," said JJ.

"He's also the main target," added Krusty. "The Macbeth Corporation wants to take him out."

"Then they will have to get to him before I do," announced Svenson thumping his fist on the table again and leaping out of the computer chair. "It seems fate as given the Svenson lineage one more chance to even the score."

"What does that mean?" asked JJ.

"It means, I'm in. All in. We'll grow the greenest, juiciest, most nutritious kale the world has ever known and then I'll personally shove it down Todhammerstein's throat."

"Excellent," said JJ.

"When do we leave?" asked Svenson.

"Tomorrow morning," said JJ.

"Cool, dudes," said Krusty. "Well, I think you two make a great team. Svenson should win the competition easily. He can get revenge for his ancestors, JJ can get back with his old girlfriend and everybody's happy. I'll hold the fort here and wait for you to come back."

"You're not coming with us?" asked Svenson.

"Nah, bro."

"Why not?"

"I can't believe I need to say this. I mean, I'm supposed to be the stoner here and even I can see a million problems with this plan."

"The plan is irrelevant," said Svenson. "No plan survives contact with the enemy. You can't plan to bring about the downfall of globalist tyranny. What is important is to be in the game."

"I'd just prefer it if the plan was a little more, umm, coherent."

"C'mon, K-man, this is not like you. You're not gonna sit here in Tittybong while there's an adventure to be had, are you?" said JJ.

"A three-man team is stronger than a two-man team," added Svenson.

"Don't you need someone to run this place while you're gone?" asked Krusty looking for any excuse to refuse.

"This plant is fully automated. It will run for a month without any human intervention."

"What about the cash stuff? Who's gonna supply Tittybong while we're gone?"

"We'll train up Sammy to do it. He was already asking me for a job," said JJ.

Krusty tried to think of more excuses but drew a blank.

"Alright, fine. Count me in," said Krusty.

"Excellent," said Svenson.

"Let's go to Sydney, boys," said JJ clapping his hands excitedly.

"Let's save the world, dudes," said Krusty ironically.

Svenson walked over and slapped JJ and Krusty on the shoulder.

"You know what time it is? It's time to fuck shit up!"

Chapter 3

Meet me in the bar at 6pm. Just want to welcome you to Sydney and debrief quickly about the competition. Regards, Florian Johansson

JJ read over the note for the umpteenth time before throwing it down on the table. He looked over to the digital clock beside the bed which read 5.43 and began pacing around the hotel room as he had been doing for the last hour. He had hoped for a quiet evening at the hotel, a time to decompress before the start of the competition the following day. Instead, he had a date with the Prime Minister of Australia who just happened to be the father of his ex-girlfriend.

The trip into the North Shore earlier that day had gone off without a hitch. The contestants driving up from Melbourne had been relieved of their car and their biometric IDs by Macbeth associates somewhere around Canberra. The car had then been driven to Macbeth headquarters near Liverpool where the genetic signatures of JJ, Krusty and Svenson were loaded onto the IDs. For the next week or so, they would be known as Paul Wochensky, Harold Blomfeld and Arnold Winfield respectively, horticultural specialists from Melbourne.

In order to fit in on the North shore, they were given appropriate clothing which consisted of slacks, dress shirts and leather shoes. The problem arose as to what to do with Krusty's hair. Whichever way you looked at it, dreadlocks were not going to work on the North Shore. Snake and Ciara had wanted to simply cut them off. Krusty's position was that he would rather cut off his left testicle. A compromise was reached where it was agreed to wrap the dreadlocks into a kind of man bun and then hide it away beneath a hat. A flat cap was deemed the most suitable option for the North Shore. In this way, the three of them were given their new identities and made presentable for the cultural milieu into which they were about to enter.

Check in at the hotel was the first big test and had gone off without a hitch. They handed over their new IDs and these became the keys to the doors to their room. The hotel itself was very luxurious containing all the things one would expect such as a swimming pool, spa, sauna, gym and other facilities. JJ had opted to take a shower and chill out in the room but no sooner had lain down on the bed to take a nap when the phone rang and the hotel receptionist advised that there was a message for him to collect.

Two primary thoughts were doing the rounds inside JJ's skull as he contemplated the meeting with Johansson. Firstly, why would Johansson want to meet with them directly? As far as JJ knew, he had no direct interest in the competition. On the contrary, one would have expected the Prime Minister to be fully tied up with other matters given that the global congress was taking place and yet he was putting aside time to meet with some lowly contestants. Was he onto them? Was it possible Amber had showed her father a photo of JJ? Could his face have been matched by cameras on entry to the city and the cops had identified him already? The second thought was whether he shouldn't just use this opportunity to tell Johansson directly that his life was in danger. That was, after all, what JJ had come to Sydney to do. But it wasn't the kind of thing you could just blurt out to a stranger. He had to build up an amount of trust before that could happen.

There was a knock at the door and JJ opened it to find Krusty and Svenson standing there in their North Shore outfits. Svenson was dressed smartly in a pink shirt and white chino combination that matched his blonde hair while Krusty looked a bit like a waiter in a white shirt and black slacks combo. He was also wearing the flat cap but, most amusingly of all, he was clean shaven for the first time since early high school when he and JJ had originally become friends. JJ couldn't hold back a grin at the sight of his friend who actually looked like the teenager that he was.

"Shut the fuck up, bro," said Krusty who pushed past JJ into the room followed by Svenson.

"There's just so little...hair," said JJ gesturing towards Krusty's head. "I wouldn't even recognise you if I saw you on the street."

"Good, it's supposed to be a disguise, isn't it. Stupid bullshit. I wish you'd never talked me into this," he said slumping down the couch. "Now what's this business with what's-his-name?"

"I assume you're referring to Johansson," said JJ. "Florian Johansson."

"Never heard of him."

"He's only the Prime Minister of this country. No reason you should have heard of him."

"What does he want?" asked Svenson.

"That's what I've been racking my brains to try and figure out. I'm worried he might be onto us but it doesn't make sense that he would personally come here to bust us. Surely he would just send the cops to do that job."

"Maybe he knows one of us. I mean, he might know the Melbourne horticulturists personally and he's coming by to say hi," said Svenson.

"Oh, shit. I hadn't thought of that. In that case we're fucked. Our cover will be blown immediately," replied Krusty.

JJ glanced over at the clock.

"Well, we're about to find out. C'mon, it's time. Let's go and meet the Prime Minister."

They headed out of the room and caught the elevator down to the second floor where the hotel's bar and restaurant were located. They were greeted by a spectacular view of the Harbour Bridge and the Opera House out of the floor-to-ceiling windows directly opposite as they entered. They walked over and took a seat by the window that was within eyesight of the front door.

"Dude, how's he going to recognise us?" asked Krusty.

"He must know us by sight or he would have arranged to meet in the lobby or at our room," added Svenson.

"If it's true that he does know the real horticulturists then we'll see him walk in, look around for a while and then walk out or sit down by himself and wait," said JJ. "If that happens, we know our cover is blown and we get the hell out of here as quickly as possible."

At the doorway there appeared a tall, handsome blonde man in a sharp grey suit and pink dress shirt.

"That's him," whispered JJ to the others.

The man scanned the bar for a few seconds before making his way towards the three of them.

"'Scuse me, gents. You don't happen to be three horticulturists from Melbourne by any chance, do you?"

"That's us," said JJ trying to sound confident.

"I figured so given there's not many other people in here. Well, you're a lot younger than I was expecting."

"Oh, really?" said JJ trying not to engage with this observation.

"How was the trip up from Melbourne?"

"Good. Yeah, good."

"Settle into the hotel alright?"

"Yep."

"Well, you're a talkative bunch, aren't you. I guess you boys prefer dealing with plants than people. Look, I won't take up much of your time. I just wanted to drop by and meet you and let you know that if you need any assistance during your stay that I'm here to help. There's a lot riding on this competition, gents, and I want to win so just reach out and I'll make it happen, whatever you need. Do you have any questions for me?"

"Umm, what do you mean by *you* want to win?" asked JJ sheepishly.

"I don't follow."

"You said that *you* wanted to win the competition."

"Me and you three together. We're a team, after all, right?"

"We're a team?"

"Of course, I'm your sponsor."

Johansson gave them a curious look.

"You are from Melbourne, aren't you? You're not just pulling my leg?"

"No, no. That's us," said JJ. "Technically, from east Melbourne. Although, he's from the west."

JJ pointed at Krusty.

"That's me. A real westie," said Krusty semi-sarcastically.

"Hey, which one of you is Arnold Winfield?" asked Johansson.

JJ looked over at the other two with a mild terror realising that he'd already forgot who was assigned to which name. Krusty's face was also showing a blank while Svenson was unresponsive.

"Forgot your own names?" asked Johansson with a raised eyebrow.

"Sorry, errr, Mr Johansson," said JJ trying to cover. "We're just a little nervous. You know, it's not every day you get to meet the Prime Minister."

"I am Winfield," announced Svenson.

"Aha, so you're the inventor of the famous Winfield Method," said Johansson.

"No," said Svenson flatly.

"You're not the inventor?"

"No."

"This is a joke, right, guys?" said Johansson who now seemed to be getting angry.

"No, no, no," said JJ quickly. "What Winfield here is trying to say is that it was a group effort. We were all involved in the development of the, umm, Winfield Method. He's just being humble, that's all. But Winfield here is the best out of all three of us. He's the one who knows the most about horticulture and hydroponics in particular."

"He's the *only* one who knows about horticulture," said Krusty under his breath.

JJ gave him a sharp kick under the table.

"Well, that's good. I've heard about the spectacular results obtained via your method and I'm hoping it will take us to victory in the competition. Look, I won't keep you any longer, gentlemen. I have to get home. My daughter is cooking me dinner tonight. Why don't you go and grab something to eat and have a few drinks while you're at it. You need to loosen up a bit. You seem a bit wooden, if you'll pardon the horticultural pun."

Johansson gave them a big smile flashing his perfect, pearly white teeth.

"Thank you, Mr Johansson. We'll do that," said JJ trying to return the smile and managing what amounted to a grimace.

"Oh, by the way," said Johansson turning as he walked away. "My office is on the top floor of the building at 12 Alice Street where the competition is being held. If you need anything urgently, just take the elevator all the way up and tell my secretary who you are. She'll make sure you get what you need. Good luck tomorrow, gents."

With that Johansson turned and walked out the door of the bar.

"Well, that was fun," said Krusty. "He actually seems like a decent bloke. Not the arsehole I was expecting him to be."

"That's because he wants us to win," said Svenson.

"Yeah, what the hell was that about? He said he was our *sponsor*."

"Sounds like the politicians are doing their usual thing of trying to take the credit for other people's work."

"Hmmm. I guess if Todhammerstein is judging the competition and he's some big vegan then the lower level players can win brownie points with the big fella by backing the winner."

"Which means the other teams will probably also have politicians as sponsors," said Svenson. "And if that's true, then the whole competition is going to be very high profile."

"Let's hope there's nobody there who will figure out that we're not the real Winfield and Co. Hey, how did you remember your name?"

Svenson held up his digital ID unit and showed the back where he had "Arnold Winfield" written.

"Good idea, bro. I'm gonna do the same thing. Hey, sounds like Amber is cooking dinner for her old man," said Krusty turning to JJ only to find him pressed up against the window looking down to the street below.

"What are you doing, dude?"

"I've gotta go," said JJ heading towards the door.

"Go where?"

"I need to follow Johansson."

"Why?"

"Looks like he's walking home. I wanna find out where he lives."

"Why?"

"So, I can find out where Amber lives."

"Hang on, bro. I don't think that's a good idea. This could kick off your Amber thing again."

"Don't worry. I'm just gonna follow him."

"Don't fuck this up, dude," warned Krusty.

JJ gave a dismissive wave as he ran to the door and skipped down the huge staircase that led to the expansive foyer of the hotel. He hurried across the white marble floor to the front door where a porter gave a small bow and opened the door for him. Down the stairs of the hotel he turned right towards the park where he had seen Johansson walking. JJ knew that Johansson lived somewhere in Kirribilli which would mean he was walking back to his house.

He hurried across the road making sure to keep what he thought was a safe distance from Johansson who had now reached the other side of the park and was crossing to a street that ran perpendicular to the park's edge. JJ was approaching the edge of the park himself when a man in a black suit with black tinted sunglasses suddenly appeared from behind a tree just a few metres in front of him. JJ stopped instinctively sensing trouble and the man pulled something out of his pocket which he held up as he walked forward.

"Agent, Richardson," said the man who was holding what looked like a police badge. "I need to see your ID."

JJ squinted at the badge to try and figure out what sort of "agent" the man was but in the heat of the moment he couldn't make it out. What he did notice was the several other men in black suits who had suddenly materialised although they were all keeping a distance. JJ realised they must be security personnel protecting the Prime Minister. He pulled the biometric ID unit from his pocket and handed it to agent who ran it over a small black scanner that he had removed from his pocket. The agent spent a moment reading off the screen.

"State your name," he instructed.

JJ's heart started to beat even harder than it had already. He racked his brain to try and remember what he was supposed to be called. He knew it definitely wasn't Winfield and he tried to visualise the other two names. Finally, it came to him.

"Wochows...umm, Wochensky," he spluttered.

"First name?"

"Pete.., umm, Paul."

"What's your business here?"

"I'm just taking a walk in the park."

"You're a visitor in Sydney?"

"Yep. I've just arrived from Melbourne."

"And where are you staying?"

"At the hotel on the other side of the park."

JJ gestured over his shoulder but the agent wasn't paying attention. Instead he held his hand up to the side of his head where JJ could make out an earpiece sitting inside the man's ear. The agent seemed to listen to something for a couple of seconds and then handed JJ's ID back to him.

"That's fine," he said before turning and crossing the road and heading down the same street Johansson had earlier.

The other men in black suits had disappeared to wherever it is that secret agents go. JJ figured it was wise not to push his luck by pursuing any further. He had gotten a rough idea of where Johansson lived. Once upon a time, the Prime Minister's official residence was nearby at Kirribilli House but that had been sold off to international interests about a decade earlier and with the decreasing status of the official head of government, the Prime Minister was now expected to organise their own accommodation which explained why he was living on a normal residential street albeit it in an exclusive suburb.

JJ decided to do a lap of the park to get this thoughts in order. It was a small park and in less than ten minutes he was back where he started. Wanting to see the name of the street which Johansson had gone down, he crossed the road from the park and looked up at the street sign. It was called George Place. He made a mental note of it before wandering a little way down the street to have a look. It was almost entirely filled with townhouses interspersed by a few low-rise apartments blocks. Expensive cars were parked in a casual fashion that revealed that this was the neighbourhood of the ultra-wealthy.

Having satisfied his curiosity, JJ turned to head back to the hotel and then froze in his tracks. Dead ahead of him just coming around the corner was Amber, her blonde hair shining in the late afternoon sun. She hadn't yet spotted him as she was looking down at her phone and by the time JJ realised he might have been able to slip by her unnoticed, it was too late. She looked up with what was at first a curious look on her face which was quickly followed by a range of other emotions that succeeded each other in short order: surprise, anger then something that JJ took for either flattery or amusement. He couldn't tell. And he couldn't move.

"JJ?" said Amber sliding her earphones out of her ears. "Is that you?"

"Yep. Hi," said JJ waving his hand like a dork and then silently cursing his own dorkiness.

"Wow, I barely recognised you. You've changed," she said gesturing to his pants and dress shirt. "You look very, ummm, North Shore."

"That's the idea. Gotta fit in."

"What are you doing here?"

"Nothing."

"Nothing?"

"I mean, I'm just out for a walk. I was just walking in the park and I saw this house over here and I thought it looked, umm, interesting so I wanted to take a closer look."

"You're into architecture now?"

"What? Umm, yeah, y'know. I like stuff. Buildings and stuff."

"So, you just happened to be in Sydney and happened to be in the North Shore and happened to be in Kirribilli on the street where I live?"

"That's right."

Amber gave him a curious, partially disappointed look.

"C'mon, JJ. Just say it."

"Say what?"

"You came looking for me."

"What? No, I didn't. Well, kind of. Yeah, I did. But, no."

"Hey, I think it's sweet," she said reaching out and touching her fingers ever so gently on the top of the JJ's hand which, combined with the smile that JJ remembered so well and her deep blue eyes made JJ's cheeks burn a little.

"How have you been?" said JJ trying to change the subject.

"Good. I'm back living with my father but I guess you knew that given that you're here. How did you know where we lived?"

"I have my sources," said JJ managing to inject a bit of confidence into his tone of voice for the first time.

"So it seems. Did you leave Tittybong?"

"You could say that. I'm here for a little while on, umm, business."

"Business? Are you and Krusty selling weed in the North Shore now?"

"No, no. Nothing like that."

"How did you get in? Security is super high cos of the big congress that's taking place."

"Like I say, I have my sources. I tried to call you. Y'know. After you left Tittybong without saying goodbye and just disappeared. But you didn't answer your phone when I called."

"Yeah, I got a new number."

"I wanted to talk to you."

"I needed some space."

"A thousand kilometres of space?"

"I needed some time to think."

"Are you still thinking?"

"I'm thinking that it's really nice to see you and that I'm glad you came looking for me."

Amber reached out and grabbed JJ's hand and this time gave a little squeeze to go with the smile. JJ smiled back and there were a few precious seconds where it was just like the old days between them. Then Amber took a glance at her phone.

"Look, I gotta go. I'm supposed to be cooking dinner for Dad and I'm running super late. Why don't I give you my new number and we can get together sometime. Y'know, when you're not working on *business*."

"I'd like that," said JJ as he pulled his phone out of his pocket and pulled up Amber's contact details.

"So, which house is yours?" he asked casually while she was typing in her number.

"I thought you knew?"

"I just know the street."

"Let's see how we go on our date and I might show it to you?" she smiled and handed him the phone.

"So, we're dating again? Just like that?"

"You don't want to?"

"No, it's just, unexpected."

"Let's see what happens. I gotta run. Bye, Jay."

"Bye."

JJ turned and watched her walk away realising for the first time that she was dressed in gym gear. He allowed his eye to appreciate the curves of her body. She turned her head briefly to catch him admiring her, gave a quick smile then flicked her head back sending her long blonde hair swinging around over her left shoulder. JJ considered just for a second following her to find out the exact location of the house but thought the better of it. There was now a more difficult but also far more enticing way to find out that piece of information. For not the first time that day, he took a long, deep breath then turned around and headed back to the hotel.

***

"Ladies and gentlemen, I'd like to officially welcome you to Kalefest, a Global Council initiative to drive forth innovation in the exciting field of hydroponic vegetable growing."

JJ, Krusty and Svenson half-heartedly joined in the round of applause which echoed around the cavernous interior of the reception hall at 12 Alice Street, Kirribilli, the venue where the kale growing competition was to take place. It was just after nine o'clock in the morning on the opening day of the competition and the contestants and various officials had been gathered for the introductory speeches. Numerous media crews were also present and cameramen and reporters found vantage points to capture the occasion. The three young men from Tittybong were marked out with a special green lanyard that they wore around their necks to signify that they were contestants. A couple of extra enthusiastic reporters had tried to interview them with lame questions about whether they were excited about the competition but they had shrugged them off saying they were trying to stay focused. Others, it seemed, *were* excited including the man at the microphone who had just been introduced as Sam Spiffo, the Australian minister for technology and innovation. Florian Johansson was also present on stage as were several other dignitaries.

"Over the next four days, we are going to find the world's foremost kale growing experts. We have teams here from around the world including the Spanish team over here to my left, the US team over here and the Japanese team just here in front. I'm pleased to announce we also have two local teams in the competition. My personal pick for the winners, although I am a little biased, is the team from Sydney over here led by Bruce Benjamin Bennings. And we also have a crack team from Melbourne featuring none other than the originator of the famous Winfield Method, Arnold Winfield, just down the back there."

All eyes in the room turned towards JJ, Krusty and Svenson. This was the moment of truth that JJ had been waiting for; the time when their cover was most likely to be blown. If Arnold Winfield was really so famous, even if it was just in horticulture circles, then there must be somebody in this room who would realise that Svenson was not in fact Winfield and that JJ was not Wochenksy and Krusty not Blomfeld. JJ rapidly scanned the faces around the room looking for any trace of suspicion, any disbelieving countenances or suspicious fingers pointing in his direction. But there were none. After a few seconds, the eyeballs turned back to the front and JJ breathed a sigh of relief. It seemed that Winfield was more known for his method than his mugshot. Maybe they would get away with this after all.

"The winning team will be placed in charge of operations for the Global Council's Keep On Kaleing program and will lead the drive to increase kale yields around the world. Kale has been identified as a critical vegetable in the Global Council's latest five-year plan and so there is no small amount of prestige to be won, ladies and gentlemen. And, of course, the winners will be presented with their prize by none other than our glorious leader and self-professed kale fanatic, Kurt von Todhammerstein. A little birdie told me that the winners may just get themselves a ticket to the closing ceremony of the congress on Friday too. So, the stakes could not be higher and I don't know about you but the nervous energy in the room is palpable. I wish everybody the best of luck and may the best vegetable win!"

Once again applause broke out as the dignitaries on stage shook hands and gathered to have their photo taken for the press. The crowd began to disperse and, as it did so, JJ caught sight of three people with green lanyards making a beeline directly to where he, Krusty and Svenson were standing. They were led by a tall, rakish man with black rimmed glasses, black hair and a supercilious expression on his face. Behind him was a red haired woman and a blonde haired chubby man. They all wore glasses and would have been in their late thirties. They strode over with chests and chins out like horticultural peacocks.

"So, which of you is the "genius" Winfield?" asked the guy in the front.

"That would be me. You got a problem, bro?" said Krusty also sticking his chin out.

"No, I am Winfield," said Svenson.

"Nah, bro. You're Blomfeld."

"Winfield!"

"Blomfeld!"

Svenson squared up to Krusty over whom he had a good six inches in height although Krusty probably had the weight advantage.

"Very funny," said the man in the black glasses who seemed to assume that the argument taking place in front of him was a joke. "It doesn't matter which of you is *Win*-field, anyway, cos you're all gonna *lose*-field. Get it?"

The man turned to his teammates who broke out into a goofy, but genuine, laughter as if the joke was actually funny.

"And who are you?" asked JJ.

"Bruce Benjamin Bennings. You've probably heard of me."

"Can't say that I have."

"I'm only the three times winner of the Sydney Horticultural Society's gold medal for excellence in the field of innovation."

"I must have missed the memo on that one."

"And you are?"

"Paul Wochensky. The blonde guy there is Winfield and the man in the cap is Blomfeld."

"Well, we finally got to the bottom of that. My colleagues here are Barbara Anne Bennetson and Arnold Bronson Anderson."

"Does everybody in Sydney have three names?" asked Krusty.

"Three is better than two."

"Well, I've got one name for all of you, bro. *Loser*."

"Hey, isn't Winfield supposed to be in his forties," squeaked Anderson in a high pitched voice that belied his girth.

"That's what I thought too," said Anderson looking Svenson up and down with a squinting gaze. "Come to think of it, you all look too young."

"That's the advantage of the Winfield Method," said JJ. "Adds years to your life."

"Keeps the skin taut," added Krusty rubbing his face like he was a model.

"Uh-huh," said Bennings who didn't look convinced. "Well, I look forward to seeing the Winfield Method in practice. Don't overdo it on the nitrogen, though. And, remember that kale needs a bit of extra potassium. But you knew that already didn't you?"

Bennetson and Anderson again chuckled.

"Attention, contestants. We will now make our way downstairs to the contest area," said an official looking person in a suit as he waved them towards a large stairwell next to the elevator on the far wall of the reception hall.

"Good luck. *Bros*," sniggered Bennings as he and the other two turned and made their way for the stairs.

"What a dork," said JJ as they followed.

The basement seemed somehow larger than the reception area. It had been partitioned into numerous room while the area in front of the rooms had been left open to create a large hall.

"You will find your names on the door to your respective rooms. Feel free to ask a staff member if you have any questions. Otherwise, please find your room and get to work. The competition begins now!" announced one of the staff.

The teams began to filter into the rooms. JJ, Svenson and Krusty walked along checking the names until they came to the very end near the wall to the right of the stairs and found a sign saying "Team Melbourne: Winfield, Wochensky and Blomfeld."

They walked inside to find a room that looked much like a mini-version of Svenson's factory. There was a single row of stands hooked together with hoses. On the far wall were a number of pipes some with taps which provided the water supply to the hydroponics system and on the side of the room was a long bench with a number of tools and bags of supplies. Svenson was like a kid in a candy store, eagerly running around inspecting the equipment while JJ and Krusty strolled around looking at names like potassium nitrate and magnesium sulphate.

"I hope Svenson knows what he's doing cos I got no idea what I'm looking at," said JJ.

"Hey, Svenson. How's it looking, bro?" asked Krusty.

Svenson was on his back underneath one of the stands checking out the hose connections. He hauled himself out and stood up.

"Excellent. It's already set up properly and I have everything I need here. I'll get to work."

"Cool, dude. Well, give us a yell if you need anything," said Krusty sitting down at a round table that had been provided for them in the front corner of the room.

He pulled out a bag of weed and began rummaging in another pocket for his cigarette papers.

"What the fuck is that?" asked JJ who snatched the bag from the table and looked over his shoulder to make sure the door of the room was closed.

"You can't smoke that here?"

"Why not? The door's shut?"

"So what? Anybody could walk in and smell it."

"C'mon, bro," whined Krusty.

"Promise me you won't smoke while you're here," demanded JJ.

"Well, what else are we gonna do? Sit and watch kale grow?"

"That's exactly what we're gonna do. For the next four days. Got it?"

"Oh, man. I'm bored already," said Krusty stretching out on the chair.

"Welcome to exciting world of horticultural innovation," said JJ sitting down beside him and realising that he too was destined for four days of boredom.

***

"Dude, let's go for lunch. I'm about to slip into a coma over here."

Krusty, JJ and Svenson were seated at the round table staring at the kale plants sitting neatly in the containers on the stands. It had taken Svenson all of about one hour to get the system up and running. Having already devised his nutrient formula in advance, he had added it to the container near the end of the row and then placed all the kale plants in their allotted containers. With the tap on and the water flowing, there was nothing more to do except sit back and watch.

"Are we able to just leave it alone?" asked JJ turning to Svenson.

"The system has enough capacity for a day's operation without human intervention," said Svenson. "Maybe two."

"So, you only have to add nutrients once per day?"

"Correct."

"But adding nutrients only takes a few minutes?"

"Correct."

"So, there's five minutes of work per day and we're here for four days?"

"Eurgh," said Krusty slapping his forehead against the table. "This is gonna be the most boring four days of my life."

"Probably," agreed Svenson. "We should buy a deck of cards or something for entertainment."

"Alright, well I guess we can afford to have a long lunch," said JJ. "Let's go and see what's around and we'll find a store to buy some cards or a board game or something to pass the time."

***

Two and a half hours later they descended back down the stairs to the basement at 12 Alice Street. Krusty, who had decided that if he wasn't allowed to smoke weed he might as well load up on beer, was feeling happy. He decided to try and slide down the handrail of the stairs but ended up almost falling on his backside.

"It's gonna be a long afternoon," sighed JJ as he watched Krusty do a poorly executed cartwheel on the way to the room before faux ninja kicking the door open.

A second later he stuck his head back out the door with a crazed look on his face.

"Svenson! Come quick, bro. We've got trouble."

JJ and Svenson ran the ten metres to the room and looked on the horrifying sight in front of them. Every one of the kale plants was flopped over in the plastic containers in which they were held like half-melted cheese sticks.

"Fuck!" shouted Svenson as he rushed over to inspect the containers. "There's no water!"

Svenson sprinted to the end of the room and frantically turned on the metal wheel that was attached to a pipe on the wall. As he did so, a gentle sound of rushing water could be heard as it made its way down the pipes and into the hoses.

“Is there anything we can do to help?” asked JJ.

“No. Just leave it to me,” said Svenson as he rushed around the system tweaking knobs and sticking his head into various nooks and crannies.

Twenty minutes later, the emergency was over. JJ was amazed how quickly the plants returned to their previous, upright state once the water was flowing again. Svenson added a nutrient formula to the system which he said would help with the stress the plants had gone through. Once it was all done, he returned the round table at the front of the room where JJ and Krusty were sitting.

“What happened?” asked JJ.

“Somebody drained the water and then turned it off from the tap. It’s sabotage.”

“Are you sure?”

“A tap does not turn itself off, does it?”

“I guess not.”

Just at that moment there was a knock at the door and a man who looked to be from the Japanese team gave a short bow before entering.

“Please, excuse,” he said. “I not here to steal information. Just want advise that I saw member of other team sneak in your room earlier.”

“Which team?” asked JJ.

“Other Australian team, I believe. Man have black glasses and is quite tall. I ask what he doing and he say he helping you. When I hear you shouting, I think perhaps he not helping at all. I no trust this man. He look, funny.”

“No, he wasn’t helping and he does look funny. Thank you very much for letting us know. Much appreciated,” said JJ as he got up to shake the man’s hand and see him to the door which he closed behind him.

“Bennings,” said Svenson.

"Motherfucker," said Krusty jumping out of his seat. "I should have nailed his smug face the first time I saw it."

"Well, if he wants to play dirty, I say we give him a little bit of eye for an eye," said Svenson.

"What are you thinking, bro?"

"It would be a shame if his kale were to have a little overdose of nitrogen," said Svenson.

"I thought nitrogen was good for plants. Is it possible to overdose on it?"

"It is possible to overdose on anything, even water."

"Alright, a nitrogen overdose it is. When are we gonna do it, though? They've probably already had their lunch."

"What about tonight? After everybody has gone home?"

"That's not gonna work," said JJ. "There's a curfew. Nobody is allowed outside after nine o'clock."

"Perfect. That means nobody will be on the street to see us. C'mon, bro. We've gotta have a little fun on this trip."

"You know what time it is? asked Svenson. "It's time to fuck shit up."

***

JJ had known Krusty long enough to know that he was as stubborn as a mule once he got an idea in his head. He made a couple more attempts to talk them out of the idea of sabotaging Bennings' system but realised it was a losing battle, especially since Svenson was all for it. Sabotaging things was something of a hobby of his from what JJ could gather. Before his move to the hills, Svenson spent most of his time as a computer hacker and was apparently one of the best in the world. Later in the evening, he put his hacking skills to use in coaxing the service elevator of the hotel into operation. The idea was to take it down to the basement of the hotel and then slip out through the carpark that way avoiding detection and ensuring their movements couldn't be traced. Svenson had already taken the liberty of hacking the hotel's security cameras as well to ensure that no footage of their movements was captured. JJ was still not happy about the idea but at least they were doing it properly and he had to admit that it would be sweet to get revenge against Bennings.

The service elevator doors slid open in front of him and Svenson gestured to enter. In a minute they were in the carpark beneath the hotel from where they slipped out and into the park across the road. 12 Alice Street was on the opposite side of the park from the hotel, near to where JJ had run into Amber the day before. There was not a single person or car in sight due to the curfew that had been imposed on the city for the duration of the global congress. They cautiously made their way towards the twenty story high building. Even though it was getting on to midnight, there were a number of lights on in the offices of the upper levels indicating that the curfew didn't apply to government employees. The plan was to enter the building through the rear door at the basement level. They had confirmed that their building passes opened the door earlier that afternoon. There was no guarantee that it would still be working at this time of night so Svenson had brought along his hacking equipment just in case they needed to do it the hard way.

They navigated to the rear of the building and Krusty skipped down the several steps that led to the back door. He held the security pass over the scanner and it flicked green. He gave the thumbs up to the others who descended the steps and into the building. The entrance door was at the other end of the building from where their room was while Bennings' room was about halfway down directly opposite the staircase that led up to the foyer. Svenson pulled out a torch he had brought along and shone it on the doors as they made their way along.

"Team Brazil." "Team Canada". "Team Britain." Finally, they got to "Team Sydney: Bennings, Bennetson and Anderson". Whoever had constructed the facilities for the competition had evidently not considered the need for door locks. That was how Bennings had been able to gain access to their room earlier in the day and how they were now going to get access to his.

Svenson was in the process of turning the handle when the lights in the hall flicked on and a male voice rang out.

"You there, freeze!"

They spun around to see a security guard descending the stairs directly opposite. He had his gun drawn and a look on his face that didn't bode well. But the look instantly softened as he hit the bottom of the stairs and he put the gun back in its holster.

"Oh, it's you, Krusty," he said in a friendly voice.

"Hey, bro," said Krusty.

"What are you doing here?" asked the guard.

"Umm, we're just down here to check on our equipment and stuff. Just wanna make sure all is good, y'know. Just a bit worried after that incident that I told you about earlier."

"How did you get in?"

"We just used our passes on the door," said Krusty gesturing towards the end of the hall where they had entered. By the way, these are my teammates, JJ and Svenson. Boys, this is McCutcheon. He's one of the security guards around here."

JJ and Svenson gave a nod to the guard.

"There's no access to the building after nine o'clock. That's the rules of the competition," said McCutcheon in a tone of voice that indicated he was telling them this purely because it was his job to do so.

"Oh, really? We didn't know, bro. Since we're here, do you mind if we just take a quick look anyway? It'll help us sleep knowing that everything's secure."

"Ok, but keep it quick. I don't wanna get into trouble. Turn off the light on your way out. There's a switch near the door where you came in."

"Thanks, dude," said Krusty as the guard turned and re-ascended the stairs.

"Quick, bro. Get in there and do your thing," whispered Krusty to Svenson once the coast was clear.

Svenson slipped into the room while JJ and Krusty kept guard out the front.

"You know that security guard?" asked JJ.

"Sort of. I met him outside this arvo while I was smoking a joint."

"You what!?"

"Nah, it's cool. He's a smoker too. I offered him a toke and we ended up choofing down two. Krusty's Special has another fan."

"I thought you agreed not to smoke for the duration of the competition."

"No. I agreed not to smoke inside. Anyway, it's lucky I did or we would have been in big trouble."

Svenson slipped back out of the room and shut the door behind him.

"All done," he said.

"Good. Let's get the hell outta here before any more of Krusty's dope-smoking buddies show up," said JJ.

"You could use a joint yourself, bro. Help you relax."

"Whatever," said JJ as he flicked the light switch off and the entrance door to the basement swung shut behind him.

***

The footage was crystal clear. It must have been shot from a camera mounted high on the wall in the front corner of the room. The timestamp in the bottom right of the screen read

00.12.23 indicating twelve minutes after midnight. The video showed the light in the room coming on and the unmistakable tall blond figure of Svenson walking straight to the bench on the wall, picking up a bag and all but emptying it into the end of the hydroponics system down the back of the room. He returned the bag to its place on the bench and then the light flicked off again. The whole thing was over in less than a minute and the video playback stopped. JJ looked over at the shit-eating grin on Bennings' face and realised he had been set up.

JJ, Krusty and Svenson had arrived at 12 Alice Street just before nine in the morning on the second day of the competition. One of the officials was waiting for them at the door to their room. He informed them they were required to report to Sam Spiffo's office but wouldn't give any more information on the matter. They took the elevator up to the top floor of the building to find Bennings already there. Spiffo was in his usual black suit seated behind a large wooden desk in a plush office. He told them a complaint had been made and then Bennings played the video. Spiffo watched it solemnly then turned to JJ, Krusty and Svenson.

"I have inspected the damage done by your actions to Team Sydney's kale crop this morning. It is extensive. As this is clearly a deliberate act of sabotage, I'm afraid I have no choice but to disqualify you from the competition. Please hand your passes to security on the ground floor on your way out of the building."

"You haven't heard our side of the story yet," said JJ.

"I don't need to," replied Spiffo. "The evidence is conclusive."

"Yeah, but the only reason we did what we did was in retaliation for what Bennings did to us earlier in the day. He sabotaged our crop too."

"Has it suffered any damage?"

"No. But that's only because we got back in time to save it."

"Please, Mr Wochensky. Do not add deceit to your list of crimes. You've brought the competition into disrepute enough as it is."

"Just ask the Japanese team. They saw him do it."

"I've made my decision and my decision is final. Now please leave this office before I have security come and remove you."

"Fuck this, bro," said Krusty and he turned to leave.

"I spit on your kale," added Svenson before JJ turned and followed the two of them out of the room closing the door behind him.

Spiffo was in on the game. JJ knew it. The whole thing was a stitch up not just to get Bennings to win the competition but so Spiffo could claim brownie points with Todhammerstein.

"This fuckin' sucks, dudes," said Krusty as he pressed the down button on the elevator.

"I am the rightful winner of this competition," mumbled Svenson. "This Bennings couldn't grow a turnip."

The elevator doors opened and they shuffled inside.

"We've failed everybody," said JJ. "Snake, Macbeth, Johansson."

Johansson! That was it.

JJ scoured the elevator side panel and finally found the button to open the doors. He pressed it furiously before the doors finally swung back open.

"What are you doing, bro?"

"Johansson," said JJ. "C'mon."

They followed JJ out of the elevator as he stalked around the area walking from room to room checking the names on doors. Finally, he decided to stick his head in an open office door.

"Excuse me. Can you please tell me where the Prime Minister's office is?"

"Back corner," was the reply and JJ rushed off towards the south west corner of the building where a secretary was sitting at a table next to the door to a large office.

"Is this the Prime Minister's office?" asked JJ.

"It certainly is," replied the woman at the desk who gave him a friendly smile.

"I'm, ummm, Paul Wochensky and this is, umm, these are my associates. We're horticulturists from Melbourne involved in the competition that's taking place down in the basement and the Prime Minister said if we ever needed help we could come to you and you would help us."

"I'll try my best, dearie. What's the problem?"

"We've been framed. I mean, we kind of got sucked into doing something stupid and now Spiffo has kicked us out of the competition."

"Well, that's not a surprise. As you may have figured out, Mr Spiffo likes to play dirty. Fortunately, we have anticipated something like this happening and Mr Johansson has made preparations for just such an eventuality. So, why don't you take a seat and tell me the details and I'll see what I can do."

"Thank you, Miss, err, Mrs...."

"Mrs Lovechild."

"Thanks, Mrs Lovechild."

"Thanks, Mrs L," said Krusty as they grabbed a seat each and proceeded to tell the story.

***

"Well, well, well. Look who's back," sneered Bennings who stood with his arms folded in the doorway of the Team Sydney room.

Bennetson and Anderson poked their heads over his shoulders like sniggering meerkats and a few other contestants also stuck their heads out of doorways to watch the spectacle of the three prodigal sons returning.

"You're not the only one with friends in high places," said JJ as he, Krusty and Svenson turned right from the bottom of the staircase and made their way back to their room at the end of the hall.

"Enjoy it while you can. Johansson won't be Prime Minister for much longer," replied Bennings.

JJ shot a look over his shoulder but Bennings and the other two had already withdrawn into the room and shut the door. What did he mean by that? JJ wondered. Was Spiffo trying to take out Johansson? Could a kale growing competition be at the heart of a battle for supremacy at the upper levels of Australian politics? It sounded absurd but no more absurd than anything else that had happened in the last two weeks.

Back in the room they were pleased to find that their kale seemed to be unharmed. Svenson gave the system a once-over and confirmed that all was in working order. Once again, there was nothing left to do but take up a position at the table and wait.

As JJ sat down, a beep emanated from his pocket and he pulled out his phone to retrieve the message. It was from Amber – *How about lunch today? Meet you in the park at 1?*

Chapter 4

"Straight flush," said Krusty turning over the two cards that sat in front of him.

JJ and Svenson groaned as they threw their cards down and Krusty started to rake in his chips. As an antidote to boredom, they had followed Svenson's suggestion and acquired a poker set from the local convenience store. Krusty had invited the security guard, McCutcheon, to join them. JJ would have thought he'd have better things to do than play a game of cards with fake money after finishing a night shift, but apparently not. Not that it mattered. He was an amicable enough guy and it was more fun to play with four players than three.

As part of the peace treaty brokered between Johansson and Spiffo after the sabotaging incidents, there was to be a permanent security patrol in the building from now until the end of the competition. In addition, locks were installed on the door of each room to allow teams to control access to their own rooms. And, to make up for the damage done to Bennings' kale crop, he had been given a kale plant from every other team as well as a set of new plants that were unadulterated. It was agreed that, in the event of a tie, Bennings' team would be awarded the win due to the losses incurred. In any case, things were back to normal, where *normal* meant sitting around waiting for kale to grow.

Svenson had begun dealing the next poker hand when JJ stood up from the table.

"Alright, I'm off for lunch."

"What? We're not invited?" asked Krusty.

"Nah, I'm, umm, I'm meeting someone."

The look on Krusty's face, one of strong disapproval, revealed that he knew exactly who JJ was talking about even though JJ hadn't told him anything about the text messages he had exchanged with Amber earlier in the day. At dinner on Monday, JJ had simply mentioned that he met Amber on the street and had refused to say much more about it but that was enough for Krusty to deduce correctly who he was meeting for lunch.

"This is not a good idea, bro."

"What's not a good idea?" asked McCutcheon who was a talkative type that liked a bit of gossip.

"JJ's gonna go on a date with his ex-girlfriend," said Krusty.

"Ooof, yeah that's never a good idea."

"It's not a date," objected JJ.

"Then what is it?"

"Ok, fine. It is a date. But it was her idea."

"So, now she wants to get back together after dumping you? What changed?"

"Like I've told you a million times, technically she never dumped me. She just left town."

"I knew this would happen. One look into her baby blue eyes and he's back in la la land. Y'know, he was lying on the couch a whole month after she dumped him," said Krusty to McCutcheon.

"Geez, she must be a special girl."

"She is a real looker, I'll give her that. All the more reason not to get your fingers burned again, I reckon."

"Thank you for the relationship advice, boys," said JJ turning to the door. "Now, if you don't mind, I've got a lunch to get to".

***

JJ poured the last of the wine into his and Amber's plastic cups. Thus far, lunch had gone better than he could have imagined. They had managed to avoid all the awkward and dangerous subjects. JJ had been funny. Amber had laughed at his jokes and praised his choice of food and wine. One of the nice things about having taken over Paul Wochensky's identity was that his biometric ID also functioned as a credit card and since JJ wasn't going to have to pay the bill he allowed himself to splurge on lunch. This wasn't hard to do in the rich enclave of Kirribilli where there were plenty of delicatessens selling high-end produce.

"So, are you gonna tell me why you're really here?" asked Amber with a mischievous look as the conversation finally turned to the risky topics.

"I told you. I came to see you."

"Originally you said you were here for work. Now you say you came to find me. Which is it?"

"It can be both, can't it?"

"Or neither?"

"So, what? We're sitting here eating lunch by random chance?"

"I dunno. Maybe you wanna abduct me or something. Maybe you joined the mob and this is all part of a ruse to kidnap the Prime Minister's daughter and hold him to ransom."

"Pretty good ruse. I hide out in Tittybong and wait for you to arrive, then date you for a while hoping you'll run home to the North Shore so I can accidentally bump into you in the street and kidnap you."

"So, you're not a secret agent trying to infiltrate the highest levels of government?"

"No. I'm just trying to infiltrate your heart."

"That's cute," Amber giggled and took a sip of her wine.

"So, what do you do all day apart from having lunch in the park with handsome men?" asked JJ.

"Nothing. Oh, god, it's so boring here. You showing up has been the most interesting thing that's happened since I got back."

"How can it be boring? This is the big city."

"Yeah, but there's all these stupid rules now and the North Shore is like its own little leper colony. It's been worse in the last week with the congress. They brought in the curfews and the armed guards everywhere all to cater to these arseholes from overseas."

"You're not a fan of Todhammerstein?"

"Who is? The guy is like a walking comic book villain."

"What does your father think of him?"

"He doesn't talk much about it but I'm pretty sure he hates him too. People like Todhammerstein hold all the real power. Our government just follows along like a little puppy dog and it seems like it's getting worse."

"Well, I wouldn't lose hope. There are movements happening. Counter-movements, I mean. To thwart the advance of the Global Council."

"I didn't know you were interested in politics? We never talked about it, did we?"

"I'm not. Well, I wasn't. But we've all been dragged into it now. You know, they cut off the money supply which means in Tittybong we now have to use black market money for everyday transactions."

"I bet there's no curfews in Tittybong though? Or police patrolling the streets. Or these weird agents and their creepy sunglasses."

"Nah, there's none of that. Tittybong does have its advantages sometimes."

"But now you're a city boy working for the man. Is that how you dress for a job in horticulture?"

Amber gestured to JJ's dress shirt.

"It's very clean. There's not even any soil involved in hydroponics, y'know, it's all water based."

"What's the name of the company you are working for?"

"Look, it's not that interesting really. It's just vegetables. Pretty boring."

"You're a man of mystery, after all," smiled Amber as she finished the last of the wine.

"Speaking of work, I think I have to get back there. Long lunches are normally the privilege of upper management. I'd love to see you again, though. For another date."

JJ flashed a cheeky grin as he began packing up the lunch.

"How about tomorrow night? We can go over to the city and check out one of my favourite clubs."

"What about the curfew?"

"This club doesn't worry about curfews. It's underground. Well hidden."

"I dunno. Can't we just do something over here. Go for dinner or something?"

"Boring. C'mon, you're a man of mystery, aren't you? You should be up for an adventure."

"Can we even get to the city? I thought the bridge would be closed."

"It is. We'll go by boat."

"Boat? Sounds dangerous."

"An element of danger just adds to the fun."

JJ didn't like the idea. He didn't like anything about the idea except the fact that it involved the beautiful girl sitting opposite him.

"Why don't you pretend you're a spy sent to the North Shore to protect the Prime Minister's daughter from the evil international bad guys."

"So, I'm James Bond."

"Exactly."

"That would make you a Bond girl."

"I'll wear my best Bond girl outfit if you agree to come."

JJ smiled.

"That's an offer too good to refuse. What time?"

"Meet at 11."

"That late?"

"Is it late? Depends if you're an international man of mystery or a vegetable grower?"

"Alright, it does sound mysterious," said JJ getting up from the table.

"I'll text you the details. See you tomorrow, vegetable man of mystery."

***

Walking back through the park JJ tried to get his mind off Amber and onto the job in front of him. He went through the course of events that was likely to occur in the next few days.

The following day, the third day of the competition, there was to be a taste test. The advice from the officials, however, was that the result did not count towards the judging of the competition. Rather, it seemed to be a purely symbolic occasion designed to pander to a handful of Global Council dignitaries. In the usual fashion of hierarchical power structures, when the boss becomes interested in something the underlings show a sudden interest in exactly the same thing. It was a handful of such underlings who were going to be the "judges" for tomorrow's event. The good thing about it, however, was that it was a dress rehearsal for the real taste test which would occur the fourth and final day of the competition. The outcome of that contributed to more than half of the final result. The practice run on the third day would give some indication of their likely chances of success which was useful information.

That led to the next consideration which was Snake and the whole Macbeth thing. Snake had said he would contact JJ on the fourth day to get an update and make arrangements for the ceremony where Todhammerstein would be present. Following the sabotage incident with Bennings, JJ had the idea that it might actually be better to lose the competition since that would mean they wouldn't meet Todhammerstein and therefore couldn't implement whatever plan Snake had in mind. The idea of throwing the competition had its merits but it would not be so easy to pull off now that there was improved security. He might be able to find a way to be alone in the room himself to sabotage their own crop but the best he could do would be to do exactly what Svenson had done to Bennings' kale. Given the rooms now had locks on the doors, it would be hard to get away with. It was also true that Svenson was hell-bent on winning meaning it wouldn't be easy to get time alone in the room.

The third issue was when to tell Amber about the danger to her father from Macbeth. A problem there was that JJ didn't know the exact nature of that danger. Without any specific knowledge about where and when an attack might happen, any warning he could give would just be a general hey-there's-a-mob-boss-after-your-father warning which was neither informative nor particularly surprising. There were probably all kinds of people and groups who had it in for Johansson. Besides which, JJ was having far too much fun re-establishing his relationship with Amber and admitting he was working for a mob boss that wanted to kill her father would probably put a damper on the romance. The long and the short of it was that there was simply far too many unknowns to make plans with any kind of certainty. He resolved not to tell Amber anything until he had information about an imminent threat to Johansson. This would almost certainly happen after the competition anyway and he would be in a better position to explain the situation then.

Back at 12 Alice Street, he skipped down the staircase and cast a glance towards Bennings' room. The door was closed as usual. Earlier in the day, he'd managed to sneak a quick look inside to get an idea of their progress. There was no noticeable difference in the size of their kale from Svenson's. Neither did any of the other teams have an advantage as far as he could tell from the glimpses he'd got here and there. At least as far as size, and therefore yield went, the competition seemed neck and neck.

As he approached the Team Melbourne room a raucous sound could be heard coming from the other side of the closed door accompanied by a familiar smell which JJ instantly recognised as Krusty's Special from the hundreds of times he had smelled it previously. He threw open the door of the room to find Krusty, Svenson and McCutcheon at the table with two others who had evidently been brought in for a game of poker. One was a Japanese team member and the other appeared to be an Italian team member if the flag on his lanyard was any indication.

"Hey, bro. How'd the date go? Get any action?" said Krusty who removed the joint from his mouth so he could have a drink of what appeared to be a glass of whisky.

"What the hell is going on here?" said JJ closing the door quickly to make sure nobody from the hall had seen inside.

"What? Same as before, bro. Just cranking out the cards. As you can see, yours truly is taking these losers to the cleaners. Oh, by the way, these are some of our international friends. There's Nakamura here and Paladino over here."

The Japanese and Italian guys gave a sort of stoned smile and a wave and then went back to helping themselves to a bag of potato chips that was half empty on the table.

"We're out of nitrogen," shouted Svenson who had removed himself from the table to go and check the condition of the hydroponics.

"JJ, can you go get some more?"

"Why me?"

"We're in the middle of a game of cards," said Svenson sitting back down at the table and picking up the deck. "I'm dealing this round."

"C'mon, Sven. Gimme something good this time you son of a bitch," said McCutcheon with the slur of a man who'd had too many joints, too many whiskies and hadn't slept for a long time.

JJ knew better than to argue with a table of drunk stoners so he turned around and left the room being sure to slip through the doorway quickly and close the door behind him to prevent any dope smoke escaping.

The nutrient supplies for the competition were tightly monitored. It was part of the judging criteria to measure yield against nutrient inputs and so teams were only given small amounts at a time which they had to retrieve from a small storeroom near the exit door of the basement where a record was kept about who used what.

"Can I get another bag of nitrogen, please," said JJ to the attendant who was seated behind a makeshift counter in the room.

"I'm sorry, Mr Wochensky. Our records show your team has used its nitrogen allocation."

"I didn't know there was a maximum amount."

"Oh, you weren't told? I'm sorry about that."

"No. I was told explicitly that we were allowed as much as we wanted because the yield would be calculated as a ratio of nutrient inputs anyway."

"Really? There must have been a change in the rules then."

The tone of the attendant's voice was dripping with disingenuity. Combined with the smirk that he couldn't hide from his face, JJ was in no doubt that this was another of Bennings' devious schemes.

"Well, I guess we'll just have to have the rules changed back then, won't we?" said JJ storming out of the room.

He was almost to the staircase when Bennings' slinked out of the doorway of Team Sydney's room with a slimy grin on his face.

"Problem, Wochensky?"

"You know exactly what the problem is, Bennings. Y'know, this is getting a bit boring," said JJ climbing the first of the stairs.

"Going to see Mrs Lovechild, are we? I'm afraid she's not in today. She's had a family emergency to deal with. And Mr Johansson is attending the workshops at the Global Council. So, I'd say you're fresh out of luck, mate."

Bennings gave what can only be described as a cackle as JJ ran up the stairs and frantically pressed the button on the elevator. A minute later he was standing in front of Mrs Lovechild's empty desk looking into the darkened office of Johansson which was locked. Whatever he was going to do, he was going to have to do it without the help of his sponsor.

He rushed back downstairs and into the Team Melbourne's room where the dope smoke was hanging thickly in the air and the volume of the racket from the poker table had increased. A loud cheer went up as Svenson won a hand and began collecting his chips from the pot.

"Svenson," said JJ rushing over to him and then tugging on the sleeve of his shirt when the Norwegian failed to respond.

"Svenson, what happens if we don't get any more nitrogen?"

"Then we're fucked," said Svenson in the boisterous tone of a man who had just won a hand of poker while being halfway through a bottle of whisky.

"We have a problem then. I don't think we can get any more nitrogen. Bennings has fucked us over again and Mrs Lovechild isn't here to help."

"What does that mean?" asked Krusty.

"It means we can't get any more nitrogen from the storeroom. They're refusing to give it to us."

"Then we'll take it by force."

"That's exactly what Bennings wants. Then he can have us arrested for assault. We've fallen for his trap once. Let's not do it again."

Svenson sat back and raised the index finger of both hands to either side of his forehead as if trying to press his skull into making his brain work. He sat in this position for several seconds.

"We must find another nitrogen source," he said finally getting up out of the chair. "What about the Japanese and Italian here," he said pointing to the two players at the table. "We can get some from their teams."

"Sharing between teams is against the rules," said JJ. "Bennings can have us disqualified for that. I think we need to find our own source."

"Hmmm," said Svenson walking around in a small circle racking his brain for ideas.

"Aha!" he proclaimed. "I've got it. Piss."

"Say again?" said JJ assuming he had misunderstood Svenson's accent.

"Piss. Urine. Wee wee," said Svenson pointing to JJ's groin as if to make absolutely sure he was being understood.

"What about it?" asked JJ.

"It's full of nitrogen. Not to mention several other nutrients."

"You want to piss in the kale?"

"Exactly."

"How are we gonna do that?"

"Like mother nature intended," said Svenson. "C'mon on."

He gestured for them to follow and JJ and the others walked to the other end of the room to find Svenson unscrewing a cap on a section of white PVC pipe that flowed into a large vessel that housed the pump that fed the liquid into the various containers down the line.

"Who wants to go first?" asked Svenson gesturing to the hole in the pipe.

"Must get back to team," said Nakamura making a beeline for the door.

"Me too," said the Italian hurrying after his Japanese counterpart.

"I'll go bro. I've been holding it in for a while and I think that whisky's catching up with me," said Krusty who unzipped his pants and sidled over to the pipe.

Forty-five seconds later Krusty let out a long groan as he zipped up his pants.

"Oh, man. I needed that."

"Who's next?" asked Svenson but he needn't have asked as McCutcheon had already stepped up to the pipe to do his duty.

"Isn't this inserting alcohol and marijuana into the plant's food?" asked JJ with a mildly disgusted look on his face as he watched proceedings. "Y'know, you lot will have marijuana and alcohol in your piss, won't you?"

"Only trace elements," said Svenson. "It might even help to stimulate growth."

"Marijuana stimulates growth?"

"It'll relax the plant, bro."

"Does kale get stressed out?"

"I'd be stressed if I was getting pissed on."

"Oh, dude, shut up. You're giving me flashbacks to Macbeth's initiation ceremony."

Fifty-seven seconds later, McCutcheon let out a long groan and zipped up his pants.

"Alright, JJ, you're next," said Svenson.

"I'll go later," said JJ. "How much nitrogen is in piss, anyway?"

"Yeah, bro. Will we have enough?"

"We might need to start drinking beers. Y'know, to increase the production," said McCutcheon.

"I'm not sure, exactly," said Svenson. "Let me do some math."

"Fuck!" said Svenson a few minutes later as he slammed his fist against the table sending some poker chips falling to the floor.

"Not good?"

"According to my calculations, we would each need to piss more than a hundred litres per day to get the required nitrogen."

"What's the maximum a human can piss in one day?" asked McCutcheon.

"A few litres?" suggested JJ.

"I'm pretty sure I pissed about ten litres once," added Krusty.

"Impossible. Your bladder would have burst," said Svenson.

"That's how it felt at the time."

"Even if you could piss ten litres, it's not enough. We need another supply," said Svenson getting up from the table where he had been doing the calculations with a pen and paper and recommencing the pacing that signified he was deep in thought.

As he was pacing his eye was once again caught by the far end of the room. JJ and the others followed him there as he began inspecting the pipes that ran down from the concrete ceiling of the basement for a couple of metres and then did a ninety-degree turn to exit the building through the wall.

"What do you see, bro?"

"There's many pipes here. Look. This one and this one are water supply but there's these others which are much wider. I think I know what they are. Let's have a look outside."

Svenson turned and strode out of the room, across the hall and out the exit door of the basement. He went round the corner of the building til he ended up on the far corner which was the section of external wall that corresponded to the location of their room. The others walked after him like ducklings following their mother.

"I knew it," said Svenson pointing to the pipes which came out through the wall of their room to the outside of the building. "Sewage pipes."

"Why do you need sewage pip...," began JJ and then he realised the answer to his question. "Oh, no, man."

"What?" asked Krusty who still hadn't figured it out.

"Svenson wants to use the sewage for the hydroponics."

"Doesn't sewage contain shit as well as piss?" asked McCutcheon.

"And toilet paper," added Krusty.

"We'll need a filter but there are already filters in the room that we can use," said Svenson.

"But won't some shit, y'know, still get through the filter."

"Shit is also a fertiliser. Why do you think gardeners put chicken shit on their garden?"

"Yeah, but this is human shit."

"Same shit, different animal."

"I don't like this idea?"

"Well, do you have another way to get your hands on a large amount of nitrogen?"

There was silence among the group.

"Good. We do it this way."

"Alright, bro. But don't expect me to help."

"You haven't been helping so far."

"That's not true, dude."

"Name one thing you have done."

"Well, I got the whisky. And the cards."

"And the dope," added McCutcheon.

"Exactly. I've been the CEO of this little enterprise."

"CEO?"

"Chief entertainment officer."

"Don't worry. I won't ask you to get your hands dirty, Mr CEO," said Svenson doing his best sarcastic voice. "As usual, just leave it to me."

A couple of hours later. Svenson stuck his head up from the pipes at the back and proclaimed success. The others tentatively walked over to take a look at the newly cut PVC pipe that connected the sewage pipe to another large container which was presumably the filter device. From there, another pipe connected into the nutrient repository.

"Time to turn it on," said Svenson.

He reached over and flicked the switch on the pump housing. An ever so quiet murmur could be heard which was quickly follow by a waft that seemed to hit the nostrils of each member of the group in unison. There was a simultaneous involuntary cry of "phew".

"Bro, that fuckin' reeks," said Krusty capturing the sentiment of the group.

"Yeah, I think it's time for me to go home," said McCutcheon holding his nose. "I'll see you tomorrow, boys."

McCutcheon walked out of the room while JJ checked the time on his phone.

"It is getting near the end of the day," he said looking for an excuse to get out. "Are we able to leave this overnight? It's not gonna blow up or something, is it?"

"It will take months to generate enough methane to create an explosion," said Svenson as if the question was the dumbest he'd ever heard.

"Cool. Let's get the fuck out here then, bro. This stench is totally destroying my buzz."

With that, the three left the room with JJ locking the door securely behind him.

***

"What is that smell," said Sam Spiffo who was standing half way up the stairs in the basement at 12 Alice Street about to give final instructions to representatives of each team about the taste test that was due to commence. Alongside Spiffo were Johansson and several of their staff. Among the group standing at the foot of the stairs were Bennings and JJ as team captains from the two Australian teams.

"It's a problem with the sewage system, sir," said JJ raising his hand to get Spiffo's attention. "The pipes run through our room at the back of the building. We've alerted building management about it but they say it will take a couple of days to fix."

This was only partially a lie. JJ had told Mrs Lovechild, who was back at work, in the vaguest of terms as a cover if anybody asked him about it. She had agreed to say that she forgot about it if anybody asked her. In this way they hoped to get through the next couple of days. Svenson had done some extra work on the filter and this had alleviated the smell in the building so that it was now more of a background nuisance than an unbearable stench.

"Fine. Hopkins, organise some air freshener or something to hide the smell when our guests arrive," barked Spiffo to one of his underlings who quickly rushed off to take care of it.

"Now, here is how taste test is going to work," said Spiffo talking to the group. "Pay attention because the official taste test that will be held tomorrow will follow the exact same process. Each team will be called up in the same order as the rooms in this basement starting from the end to my left. Thus, Argentina will go first and all the way along until we get to Team Melbourne who will be last. When called on, you are to lay a single leaf of kale on the plate of each judge. You are not to speak unless spoken to and you are to wear your mask at all times. Any questions? No? Good. Our guests are due to arrive in ten minutes so I suggest you get your three best leaves ready right now."

With that, the various contestants hurried off to their respective rooms to get organised. JJ was just about to do the same when he noticed Johansson was trying to make eye contact with him. He gave a hand signal to indicate that he wanted JJ to wait. JJ moved over to the side while Johansson finished talking with an official before making his way down the stairs.

"How we looking, Mr Wochensky?"

"Really good, sir," said JJ.

This was not a lie. To the amazement of JJ and Krusty, and the disbelief of even Svenson, their kale had grown like crazy overnight. Whatever was in the sewage was certainly doing something very special. Each plant had almost doubled in size from the previous afternoon. On yield alone, they now had a huge advantage. As to the taste, none of them were game enough to try the kale for themselves and so the outcome of the taste testing session was of extra interest. Based on the deep green colours and the juiciness of the leaf, Svenson had deduced that the taste should be exceptional but the judges would be the true test of that.

"Excellent. The Winfield Method is paying off, is it?"

"It's working better than we could ever have hoped."

"Glad to hear it. Now, a word of advice. If the taste test goes well, we can be sure that Spiffo and Bennings will put out all the stops before the final judging tomorrow. That means the potential for more sabotage. So, I need you to be extra vigilant about protecting the produce. I'd like to ask you that you stay in the room overnight tonight just so we can be one hundred percent sure of no funny stuff. I've organised for security to turn a blind eye to your presence in the building and I'll have Mrs Lovechild organise some food and beds for you so you'll be comfortable in the room. What do you say?"

"Sure," said JJ with as much enthusiasm as he could muster knowing that the request was not really optional but also with an eye, or rather a nose, to the raw sewage that was currently being pumped into the room.

"Outstanding. Good luck with the taste test."

"Thank you, sir," said JJ heading back to the room.

***

About fifteen minutes later, all teams were assembled in the hall. The team members not directly involved in the taste test had been asked to stand in a group near the exit door to the left of the staircase. The judges were to sit at three tables and chairs that had been set up directly opposite the stairs near the door to Bennings' room while the team members who were going to serve the kale were lined up in a straight line to the right of the table. Each team representative was carrying a small plastic container with their three best kale leaves and a small utensil for serving. Everybody in the room was wearing masks over their mouths and noses as per the protocol required for dealing with members of the Global Council. Only Spiffo and Johansson were exempt. Also exempt were the judges themselves who descended the stairs and were greeted by Spiffo and Johansson in turn. They were in late middle age and, as Krusty observed under his breath to Svenson, looked like their regular diet consisted more of pork than of kale. The two men and one woman sat down with a regal air in their allotted places.

"Ladies and gentlemen, we will now begin the taste test. Starting with the team from Argentina," announced Spiffo.

Spiffo gestured to the first contestant who stepped forward and plopped a single leaf of kale on each judge's plate before standing expectantly off to the side to await the response. The judges each picked up the knife and fork that was beside their plate and daintily cut off about a three inch squared section which they placed carefully into their mouths before performing an elaborate and conspicuous mastication manoeuvre that lasted several seconds.

"Not bad."

"A bit floppy but otherwise tasty."

"Yes. It needs a crisper texture but the taste is acceptable."

The three judgements given, the Argentinian member nodded his acceptance and returned to his teammates off to the left. The process moved forward without a hitch through the Botswanan, Chilean, United States, British and German teams before Bennings' was called on. He stepped forward and gave an obsequious bow to the judges before placing the kale leaf on each plate while bloviating about how the kale was "hand grown" and "nurtured with care" in flagrant disregard of the rule not to speak unless spoken to. JJ shot a look in the direction of Spiffo who made no sign of acknowledging the breach while Johansson, who was standing next to his colleague, gave JJ a small shake of the head to signify not to make a fuss.

The judges took a bite and then burst out into enthusiastic praise. "The best kale I've ever tasted", a "masterpiece," "the work of expert artisans". Bennings' beam of pride was only exceeded by the delight on Spiffo's face. Bennings took another bow and then joined his teammates who gave him some enthusiastic pats on the back.

So it went until the Japanese contestant gave a more culturally appropriate bow leaving JJ to finish the proceedings. He stepped forward carefully and placed a leaf on the plate of the first, second and then third judges. A murmur arose from the other contestants as he did so. Even from a distance, the superior size and greenness of the leaf he placed on each plate was patently obvious. Spiffo held out his hand to the group to signal for silence. The gossip died down.

“Oh, my. That’s the biggest one I’ve ever seen,” said the female judge.

“She needs to get out more,” whispered Krusty to Svenson.

JJ stood and awaited the verdict which came quickly and unanimously.

“Splendid. Absolutely splendid.”

“A clear winner.”

“Best kale I’ve ever tasted by some margin.”

JJ’s face lit up and he also bowed although more out of jubilation than anything else. Johansson stepped forward with a huge smile on his face and gave JJ a thumbs up before addressing the crowd.

“Thank you very much, ladies and gentlemen. An excellent result and one that gives every team something to strive for between now and the official judging tomorrow.”

With that, matters were at a close. Johansson and Spiffo posed for photographs with the judges before escorting them up the stairs. JJ gave Krusty and Svenson a high five.

“Well, that gives new meaning to the phrase *eat shit*,” said Krusty.

“I don’t know how to explain it logically,” said Svenson. “But we seem to have stumbled upon something that works better than the existing technology.”

They headed back to their room and JJ noted the furious faces of Bennings, Bennetson and Anderson.

“I think we’re about to put the *win* in Winfield Method,” he said loudly their direction.

Bennings turned and stormed into Team Sydney’s room closely followed by the other two. JJ still wasn’t sure whether winning the competition would be a good thing but for now it felt good to be the hot favourite.

***

Amber had texted JJ that afternoon to tell him to meet her at 11pm underneath a rail bridge at McMahon's Point. JJ had reservations about leaving Krusty and Svenson alone in the room but his decision was made easier by the fact that Svenson appeared to have been swept up in the proceedings and was now exhilarated by the fact that his kale was almost certain to win. He vowed to guard the kale with his life and JJ didn't doubt that he would do just that. As for Krusty, JJ was well aware of his ability to stay up all night smoking weed, drinking whisky and playing poker. He'd seen him do it many times and had even joined him on a couple of occasions. He got some ironic comfort in the fact that the smell of sewage would provide a useful cover for the smell of dope smoke that might have attracted unwanted attention. Finally, there was McCutcheon who was back on night shift and was only too happy to join in the fun. Having the security guard in the room itself was another bonus.

If he was confident about the security on the home front, he was less confident about the trip he was about to take. As he stood waiting for Amber, who was late, his thoughts turned to some of the inherent risks. Being out after curfew and venturing into the city proper both made a run in with the boys in blue more likely. If that happened, the police might decide to dig a little deeper than the data on his biometric ID and find out who he really was. There was a non-zero chance he would blow his cover.

Such reservations evaporated into thin air as soon as he caught sight of Amber walking around the corner of the laneway that led beneath the bridge. Her outfit might have been the exact opposite of the frilly long white dress she wore the day before. For one thing, it was all black. For another, there was far less of it. She wore black boots, black shorts and a tight black crop top that left her midriff exposed. Black lipstick added the final juxtaposition to her long blond hair. The overall effect was part gothic, part army cadet.

"Is that what you're wearing?" she asked as she approached JJ who was still dressed in his North Shore costume.

"It's all I've got," he said.

"Well, you're gonna stand out like a, ummm, like an office worker in a gothic nightclub."

"I didn't realise we were going to a nightclub."

"You thought we were gonna go for tea and scones at midnight in the city after curfew?"

Amber laughed as JJ struggled to think of what to say.

"I think it's cool. You'll be showing everybody that you don't give a fuck. That's rock'n'roll. C'mon, we've gotta hurry. I'm late and we're about to miss the boat."

Amber grabbed JJ's hand and they hurried through a series of backstreets until they reached a cliff face that fell down into the Harbour below. Amber ushered them through a hole in a chain wire fence that allowed access to a rocky, but clearly well used pathway that fell steeply down to a small clearing that couldn't have been more than a few metres wide and which functioned as a kind of natural jetty.

"Damnit," said Amber checking the time on her phone. "We might be too late."

But her fears were instantly dispelled by the sound of oars against water and like the ferryman of Hades the figure of a man appeared standing upright in a small dingy that was not much more than six feet long. The man didn't say a word but brought the vessel in parallel the shore and grabbed on to a chain which JJ hadn't even realised was there to pull the boat against the edge of the rockface. Amber stepped confidently into the vessel as if she'd done it a million times before. She sat down in front while beckoning to JJ to take the rear seat. With far less confidence, JJ managed to get himself into the boat without falling overboard. Once his passengers were safe, the boatman pushed away from the shore and began rowing the couple of hundred metres to the other side with the Harbour Bridge in full gothic splendour that seemed to match Amber's outfit hanging pitch black against a grey sky to their left.

The trip was over quicker than JJ expected and they jumped out of the boat on the other side without saying a word to the boatman. Amber led JJ through a small park and then over a narrow street and around the corner to their left where another set of stairs led straight down below street level. As the Harbour Bridge disappeared from sight beneath a concrete wall to his left, JJ could just start to hear the low rumble of loud music which became louder and louder as they descended even further so that they must have been about two stories below grade when they came to a large metal door which Amber banged on twice. It was immediately opened and a large man with a shaved head gave a knowing nod and let them inside.

The low rumble was now a loud racket which emanated from a stage directly opposite the door as a heavy metal band played with flashing lights and what looked to be a mock goat's head mounted on a pole. The audience, all dressed in black, seemed to be enjoying the entertainment. Amber led JJ to the left around the back of the crowd and through an adjoining room into a larger room where the noise from the band no longer registered on the Richter scale but was at a volume that allowed conversation to happen. Groups of people were mostly seated in what was essentially a pub with a bar to the right and some pool tables at the back. Amber scanned the area and saw a seated man waving for her attention. He had black frizzy hair and wore a leather vest with numerous patches attached to it and a t-shirt with the sleeves cut off revealing well sculpted biceps. JJ also noticed a large scar down the outside of the man's arm which looked to be a knife wound. His face also appeared to be wounded although whether it nature or nurture was hard to tell.

"Who's the doofus?" was his initial greeting to both Amber and JJ.

"This is my friend, JJ."

"Hey, hey, JJ. You look like you've stepped straight out of a hard day at the office."

"Actually, I kind of have," said JJ in what was an overly friendly response that drew malicious smiles from the other members of the table.

"What's the deal bringing your North Shore buddies where they don't belong, Amber?"

"What? No. JJ's not from the North Shore. Actually, he's from the bush."

"The bush, is it?"

"Yep. Tittybong born and bred," said JJ, again his friendly tone again appearing as weakness in the eyes of the leather clad dwellers of the bar.

"So, you live in the bush, you're dressed like a yuppy from the North Shore and you're visiting a gothic club in the city? You're a bit confused, aren't you, JJ?"

"Give him a break, Cody," said Amber sitting down at the table and gesturing for JJ to sit next to her.

"What are you doing here, JJ?"

"I'm starting to wonder that myself," said JJ as he pulled a seat from nearby and dragged it to the table.

"JJ is my guest here," said Amber. "Maybe you could at least not treat him like total shit."

"Alright, just partial shit then," said Cody to sniggers from the others.

"Tell me this then, JJ, since we were just talking about it when your arrived, what's your opinion on the Global Council."

"I hate them," said JJ sincerely.

"Hmmm, maybe you're not such a doofus after all. Why do you hate them?"

"It's because of them that the future of Tittybong is under threat. With the cash ban and the ban on the movement of people, places like Tittybong are going to suffer very badly."

"Ok," said Cody nodding as if impressed by the obvious passion in JJ's voice. "Now what if you could do something about it?"

"Whaddya mean?"

"You know the Global Council is meeting right now in the North Shore and I take it you just came from the North Shore since you're wearing the North Shore uniform and you're with a North Shore resident. So, you have, *we* have, a once in a lifetime opportunity to do something about it."

"Like what?"

"Like assassinate Todhammerstein and some of these other fuckers."

"Wouldn't work. They'd just get new fuckers to fill the roles."

"Maybe. But maybe the new fuckers would think twice about banning cash and other things like that if they knew they had something to lose out of the deal."

"That's not how it works in the real world. In the real world an external threat hardens supporters of an ideology against the enemy."

"What are you a fucking sociologist? Professor JJ?"

"What you need to do is destroy the ideology that underpins the whole thing. That's the only way to make lasting change."

"You sound like you've actually thought about this," said Amber who seemed impressed by the way JJ was handling himself.

"It has crossed my mind once or twice," JJ smiled.

"Bunch of airy-fairy bullshit if you ask me," said Cody. "Ideology doesn't mean shit. People do. Get rid of the people and you solve the problem. That's what we're gonna do."

"You're gonna assassinate Todhammerstein?"

"That's the plan."

"Are you back on this again, Cody?" said Amber.

"Yes I'm back on this. I'm back on this cos the man is only a few kilometres away from where we sit right now. Here's here for only a few days and we're sitting down here like chumps."

"So what?," said Amber. "You'll never get anywhere near him. You so much as show your face on the North Shore and they'll arrest you. It's a pipe dream."

"It's got more chance than Mr Ideology over. Did your mommy choose that shirt for you, Professor JJ?"

"Ok, that's it," said Amber getting up from the table and pulling JJ up with her. "I thought you could at least be civilised with my friend but obviously I was wrong."

"Do I look civilised to you, babe?"

Cody and the others at the table laughed as Amber led JJ into an adjoining room which was smaller than the last but with less people. They took a place in the corner on a small table with two chairs beside it.

"Those friends of yours are dicks," said JJ as he sat down opposite Amber.

"Yeah, sorry about that. But did you mean what you said about the Global Council?"

"Absolutely."

"I always thought you were just some happy go lucky pot-head. But the way you spoke before there was real passion in your voice. I'm impressed."

"What about you then?" asked JJ. "You've got a dark side I didn't know about hanging around down here with a bunch of lowlifes."

"They're ok. Their heart is in the right place. Well, most of them. I don't know if Cody has a heart. But the enemy of my enemy is my friend, as the saying goes."

"So, you hate the Global Council too?"

"Are you kidding? They didn't just destroy Tittybong. Look at this place. We have to creep around like criminals just to do things that would have been perfectly normal once upon a time. You can't even go for a walk without the agents harassing you. This is not the way for a human being to live. Even Cody knows that."

"Seems like we've got more in common than we thought," said JJ.

"I'm starting to think you really are an undercover spy," said Amber with another of her mischievous smiles.

"Well, if I'm James Bond and you're a Bond girl, then we should probably be doing less talking and more of this."

JJ leaned in slowly and placed his lips on Amber's.

"Being a good kisser is another thing we've got in common," said Amber as she opened her eyes.

"Let me get us a drink," said JJ getting up to go to the bar.

"No," said Amber. "It's not right. You being here. Us being here. Let's go somewhere else."

"Where else can we go? It's after curfew, isn't it? Or are there other dingy clubs we can try?"

"Let's go back to the North Shore."

"Is there something open there? I thought everything was shut."

"We can go back to my place."

Normally this sentence and the tone of voice with which it was delivered would have been music to JJ's ears but he knew there was a problem.

"Won't your father be there?" he asked.

"No. He said he's gonna have to pull an all-nighter. Something to do with the Global Council stuff. He said he needs to be in his office in case something goes wrong. I dunno. I wasn't paying attention. Point is, we'll have the house all to ourselves."

JJ took a second to think about it.

"C'mon, Mr Bond. You're not going to deny your Bond girl, are you?" said Amber standing up and whispering in his ear pushing her body against his as she did so.

JJ didn't need any more convincing.

"Lead the way, madam," he said in his best British accent and Amber and he left the noise of the club behind.

Chapter 5

JJ was awoken by a beeping sound from his phone signifying he'd received a message. The sweet smell of Amber's hair wafted into his nostrils and the warmth of her back reminded him of the pleasures of the night before. He wanted nothing more than to continue to lie in that blissful state but the worries of the world barged their way into his consciousness. The competition. Krusty and Svenson left to their own devices in the room overnight. And, more urgently, the time. He'd forgot to set an alarm and it must have been three or four in the morning before he and Amber finally went to sleep which meant it could easily be midday for all he knew. What if the message was from Krusty telling him the taste test was about to start?

He opened his eyes and swung the arm that had been around Amber's waist over to the bedside table where his phone was. The time was 8.59am. That was good. But the message was from Snake and that was bad. It read:

Meet me at the pergola in the park opposite 12 Alice Street in 30 minutes. Don't be late.

JJ had been expecting to hear from Snake but the message was still a major downer and not just because he'd rather stay in bed. He ran back over the likely sequence of events in his head. It seemed they were going to win the competition. They would find out for sure at around midday when the official taste test was conducted. The winners would get to meet Todhammerstein tomorrow. That was when JJ would have to implement whatever Snake's plan was. If it worked, Todhammerstein would be dead and Macbeth would move to the second part of the plan which involved Johansson. JJ didn't know much about political intrigue but he figured Macbeth would probably move fast to capitalise on the element of surprise. Then again, maybe she would lie low and wait for the globalists to leave town.

All of this raised the still unresolved problem of when to tell Amber about the danger to her father. He could do it now, of course, but Snake's message didn't leave much room to move. He'd have to be out of here in about ten minutes to make it to the park in time. He couldn't just drop a bombshell like that and then run out the door. He'd have to do it later that day when he would have more time to explain things clearly and maybe even tell her the truth about why he was in the North Shore.

These thoughts were interrupted by a loud thud that came from downstairs which sounded like a door closing. It was followed by the unmistakable sound of Johannson's voice calling up the stairs:

"Amber, are you up?"

"Almost, Dad," said Amber rousing from sleep and stretching her arms out in front of her as she rolled over onto her back.

JJ had already sprung out of bed like a frightened monkey and was frantically throwing on his clothes which were scattered about on the floor.

"What are you doing?" said Amber rubbing the sleep from her eyes.

"I'm getting out of here, that's what," whispered JJ as he wrestled to get his shoes on and fumbled while trying to tie them up.

"Why?"

"Cos your father's home, that's why."

"What? Nah, don't worry. He'll be cool about it. Besides, I want you meet him," said Amber sliding out of bed and slipping into her dressing gown.

"I can't meet him," said JJ as he ran over to the window and flung it open.

He stuck his head out to find that it was a two-story drop straight down. He'd have a choice between landing on a barbecue, a mountain bike or one of the concrete steps that led down into the small backyard. It looked like a choice between a broken leg, a broken arm or a broken back. Perhaps all three at once.

"What is this, the 1950s?" said Amber as JJ turned back to the inside of the bedroom. "Relax. He's not going to throw you off the Harbour Bridge or anything."

"I'd just, I'd rather not meet him, that's all," said JJ trying to be calm. "He's the Prime Minister, after all."

Amber gave him a quizzical look but decided not to press the matter any further.

"Ok. Let's see if we can slip you out the front door then. It's the only way out. Unless you'd like to jump out the window?"

"No. The door is fine."

Amber opened the bedroom door and they walked out into the upper balcony of the townhouse which looked down over the large and ornate staircase that led down to the ground floor. JJ could see the front door from where he stood and half considered jumping over the bannister but he followed Amber down the second flight of stairs that led back towards the interior of the house and came out facing a small corridor that ran into the kitchen. He was just a few metres, just a few seconds, away from the door with the goal in sight when Johansson heard the soft patter of footsteps and stuck his head around from the kitchen.

“Wochenksy?” he said with a furrowed brow that signified consternation and surprise.

“Morning, sir,” said JJ who felt like his heart was going to jump out of his chest.

Johansson put down whatever he was holding and stepped into the hallway to see Amber standing behind JJ.

“What are you doing here? I mean, why aren’t you back in the room? You promised you’d stay the night.”

This was not the line of questioning JJ expected from a man who had just caught his daughter trying to smuggle her lover out of the house.

“It’s fine, sir. The other team members stayed the night and the security guard was there with them. The room is in safe hands, I can assure you.”

“Well,” said Johansson as if appeased by the explanation. “I guess that’s ok. But you better get back there quickly to prepare for the final judging today.”

“My thoughts exactly, sir. I was just rushing out the door to do that.”

“Very good. Off you go then.”

JJ couldn’t believe his luck. He took two steps closer to the door when Amber’s voice rang out.

“Excuse me. Don’t you want to meet my guest properly?” said Amber to her father.

“We already know each other,” said Johansson.

“I mean, don’t you want to know why he’s here. He’s here because of me, you know?”

“He is? That’s right. So? What? You two are an item, are you? But you’ve only been in town a few days, Wochensky.”

“That’s right, sir,” said JJ. “Your daughter and I, I mean, Amber and I, we, umm, we met in the park just nearby the office. I was out for a walk one afternoon and we just bumped into each other.”

"Well, how nice. We can talk about it more later. Wochensky has work to do, dear."

Amber's cheeks burned a bright red with anger.

"Wochensky has work to do, does he?"

The tone of her voice sent a chill down JJ's spine. It was the voice of a woman who had just uncovered a big, bad secret.

"Why are you angry?" asked Johansson.

"You're right. I should calm down," said Amber who took a couple of deep breaths.

A weird smile came over her face that was even worse than the anger from JJ's point of view.

"So, how do you two know each other?" Amber asked her father.

"Wochensky here is one of the hotshots from Melbourne who I invited up to take part in the horticultural competition that is currently taking place as part of the Global Congress. A competition it looks like we are about to win. Right, Wochensky?"

"You bet, sir," said JJ.

"And if we win, I'll be presenting Wochensky and his teammates to none other than Kurt von Todhammerstein tomorrow afternoon."

"I see," said Amber. "So, you're from Melbourne are you, Wochensky? Whereabouts in Melbourne?"

"One of the inner suburbs," said JJ who raised his eyebrows to signal to Amber to end the conversation.

"Which one?"

"One of the eastern suburbs."

"What's the name of it?"

"Amber, for god's sake, Wochensky hasn't got time to stand around here talking about the geography of Melbourne. He needs to get back to the competition."

"Your father's right," said JJ. "I should go. See you later, sir."

"Let me see you out," said Amber as she followed JJ to the front gate.

"Are you gonna tell me what the fuck all that was about?" said Amber pointing back inside the house.

Her angry face had returned.

"I can't right now," said JJ holding up both hands in a gesture of calm. "But I will later on, I promise. Let's meet up this evening and I'll tell you everything."

"So, let me get this straight," said Amber ignoring his plea. "You've been pretending to be a horticulturist from Melbourne for the last three days. Not just any horticulturist but one who's involved in a global competition sponsored by the Prime Minister of the country?"

"Yes, but that's just part of the story."

"So, you didn't come to Sydney to find me? Hah, I should have known."

"No, I did," said JJ grasping Amber on both shoulders. "Amber, I did come to find you. The competition thing is just a ruse."

"Doesn't sound like a ruse to me. Sounds pretty serious. And you're about to win and meet Todhammerstein himself."

"Yes. That's all part of it. But I came to see you first and foremost."

"Hang on. You're going to meet Todhammerstein? When is that happening?"

"Tomorrow if all goes to plan. But forget about that. I've gotta go now but let's meet tonight and I'll tell you all of it right from the start. The whole crazy story."

Amber wasn't listening. All of a sudden, she seemed deep in thought. JJ checked the clock on his phone.

"Amber, I've got to go."

"If you've got access to Todhammerstein, then we can take him out," said Amber.

"What do you mean take him out?"

"Cody. Remember Cody from last night? All he needs is an opportunity; a way to get near Todhammerstein."

"I thought you didn't like Cody?"

"I don't. But I like his idea. Killing Todhammerstein could get us all out of this mess."

"No, it won't. Like I said last night, it's the ideology that needs to die. That's what I'm here for. To kill the ideology."

"What does that mean?"

"I told you, I don't have time to explain now but I'll explain later. Trust me."

"Trust you? After you've been lying to me for three days straight?"

"I'm sorry. I couldn't tell you the truth at first cos it would threaten the mission."

"Because of my father?"

"Exactly."

Amber didn't look convinced but JJ was out of time.

"I've gotta go. I'll text you later to set up a time to meet. Ok?"

"Ok."

JJ leaned in a gave Amber a kiss on the cheek before rushing off in the direction of the park.

***

Snake looked like a tourist dressed in a white dress shirt and a white bowler hat with mirrored sunglasses that reflected JJ back to himself as he sat down next to him on the bench seat that ran around the edge of the pergola in the park opposite 12 Alice Street.

"Morning, Snake."

"It is a good morning, isn't it, Mr JJ? The sun is out. The birds are singing. Did you have a nice sleep-in at the Johansson residence?"

The blood froze in JJ's veins. He realised in an instant what should have been so obvious. Macbeth had Johansson under surveillance. And that meant Snake had Johansson under surveillance. JJ had forgotten all about that fact and the mistake was enormously costly. By showing up there he had inadvertently revealed everything. Whoever was surveilling the property must have already told Snake about the previous night's liaison. Hell, Snake probably had photographs of the whole episode. JJ tried to remember whether the blinds in Amber's room had been closed or not. He couldn't recall. There was now a possibility that Snake had photographs of JJ and Amber in flagrante. But even worse than that was the fact that Snake knew about the two of them.

"Yes," was all he could think to say.

Snake slid his sunglasses down his nose and looked over the frames as he leaned over and gave JJ a cold stare. He spoke in his serious voice.

"Now, Mr JJ. If you want to get a little pussy on the side, that's fine by us. We're not prudes at the Macbeth Corporation as I'm sure you'll agree. Nevertheless, this incident does raise a question of your loyalties. I need to know that they sit one hundred percent with the Corporation. Can you give me that assurance?"

"Absolutely, Snake. One hundred percent."

"Good. Now specifically in relation to the mission, we need you to be focussed. Therefore, you are not to see Ms Johansson until after the meeting with Todhammerstein tomorrow. Understood?"

"No problem," said JJ who knew that it would be a problem.

Snake leaned back on the bench and slid his sunglasses back on. He resumed his normal casual tone of voice.

"Excellent. We'll say no more about it then. How's things going with the competition?"

“Not very good, I’m afraid. I’d say we’re in with an outside chance but there’s been some setbacks. As you know, growing kale is not our specialty.”

“Really, Mr JJ? Cos my information is that you’re raging favourites to win. I’m told you’re so far ahead of the competition that the other teams have given up.”

“Who’d you hear that off?”

“Mr JJ, we have people in many places. Not just out the front of Johansson’s house.”

JJ racked his brain to think who the informant could be. The only option seemed to be a plant in one of the other teams. Could it be Bennings? That didn’t make sense as he was allied with Spiffo. And then he realised who it was: McCutcheon. Of course! He should have known. A security guard who spent most of his time smoking dope and hanging around even when he wasn’t working. It didn’t make sense at the time but it did make sense now. McCutcheon was the plant.

“Well, it’s a subjective judgement, I guess,” he said trying to cover his lie as best he could. “My perspective is that we’re not favourites but others can have their own view.”

“Ok. We’ll proceed as if you are going to win, Mr JJ. As you know, the winners will have the high privilege of meeting the old kale enthusiast himself, Kurt von Todhammerstein tomorrow around lunchtime. Todhammerstein will be addressing the congress the following day including giving a live speech that will be broadcast around the world. I’m sure you remember our plan. Here is your weapon to put that plan into action.”

Snake reached into the pocket of his dress pants and pulled out a small white plastic bottle that was about the length of his hand. He handed it to JJ who saw that it had a spray nozzle on top but otherwise had no markings or label. It looked like the kind of thing you could buy in any supermarket.

“What’s this?”

"As you no doubt recall, Mr JJ, the plan here is to infect Todhammerstein with a cold virus. The cold virus is in that container. In fact, there's a whole host of different cold viruses so we can maximise our chances of success."

"They're in the water?"

"It's not water. It's a special fluid conducive to keeping viruses activated and for transmitting them into the face of others."

"Sounds very hi-tech."

"Do I detect a hint of scepticism in your voice, Mr JJ?"

"No. It's just, I 'm no virologist, but I would have expected something a little more sophisticated."

"You're right, Mr JJ. You're not a virologist. And you're job is not to ask questions but simply to execute the Corporation's requirements. In this case, you simply have to get within spraying range of Todhammerstein and spray as much of the contents of that bottle as you can. You don't have to spray it straight into his face. Although, if the opportunity presents itself you can certainly do so. You need to spray it anywhere in the vicinity as long as it's within thirty seconds of him walking through."

"How am I gonna get away with that? You know what they're like. They lock everything down like a prison cell. If I go spraying weird stuff into the air, I'll be tackled to the ground in one second flat."

"Use your imagination, Mr JJ. Pretend you're nervous and it's your deodorant bottle. Or pretend it's air freshener and you're trying to make a good impression. Whatever you need to do to make it happen. That's your part of the mission. My mission is to give the bottle to you and give you your instructions. Now, I suggest you get back to the competition and make sure that we get the result we need. If you need any assistance between now and the big event tomorrow, you've got my number and I'm happy to help. We all want this plan to succeed, don't we?"

"Yep."

Snake got up and began to walk away before stopping and turning around.

"And just remember, Mr JJ, we have eyes on you at all times."

Snake left the park and JJ sat there for a while to gather his thoughts. He looked at the plain white bottle and shook his head. They weren't even trying to make it look legitimate. There was probably nothing more than water inside. On the other hand, he didn't fancy taking the lid off to find out just in case there was something nasty in there. He was well and truly trapped now. There was no backing out. He would have to proceed and make the best of it. He got up and walked across the road to the basement of 12 Alice Street.

***

He knew it was bad before he even saw it. The door to the Team Melbourne room was wide open and the now familiar smell of weed and whisky combined with shit and piss was present in the hall itself. Out the front of the door, several competitors from other teams loitered some with whisky glasses, some with beer bottles, a couple even smoking on a joint. It looked like a college dorm party.

Inside the room it was even worse. There must have been more than a dozen people hanging around. Krusty was still at the card table. Even by his standards, he looked zonked out like a car that had run out of fuel rolling the last few metres before it stopped altogether. Svenson looked more alert. He was holding court over in front of the hydroponics setup apparently giving some technical advice to a few other competitors who were standing around.

"Nitrogen sulphate can't be used in that scenario, my friend. Besides which, it would throw out your pH levels and everything would turn to shit."

If the Winfield Method was anything to go by, turning things to shit sounded like a good thing, thought JJ to himself ruefully. He wondered if the people Svenson was talking to knew that there was shit running through the very system they were standing in front of. It was then he caught sight of the kale plants. They were huge. Clearly the shit had continued to work its magic. The plants seemed to have doubled in size again overnight. JJ had no idea how big kale plants were supposed to grow, but he was pretty sure they weren't supposed to get *that* big.

JJ gave a loud sigh like a school principal called in to discipline the students. First thing he had to do was to get the people out. He walked over to the card table and waved his hands to get Krusty's attention.

"Krusty," he shouted over the noise. "Oi!"

JJ walked over and tugged on Krusty's sleeve. The bloodshot eyes of his friend eventually showed some level of recognition.

"Hey, bro," said Krusty as if he were sleep talking.

"I need to talk to you," said JJ pulling on Krusty's shirt to signal for him to get up.

Krusty slowly complied.

"Nakamura, your turn to deal, bro," he said throwing the cards to the Japanese competitor as he followed JJ out of the door and over near staircase where there was a modicum of quiet.

"What the fuck is going on here, man?" whispered JJ.

"What's the problem, dude?"

"The problem. We've got multiple problems. So many problems I don't know where to start. Let's start with all these fuckin' people in our room. Why are they in there?"

"It's a victory party, bro."

"We haven't even won yet."

"You don't understand, dude. Have you seen the size of that kale in there. It's huge. It's about three times bigger than anybody else. All the other contestants have given up. They know they can't win. So we invited them in for a celebration."

"What if they figure out how we're doing it. With the shit and the piss and stuff. They'll disqualify us."

"Nah, it's cool. Svenson just made up something about the Winfield Method. They all bought it."

"Ok. Let's pretend that's true. Why is every person in the room smoking a goddam joint?"

"This is the hilarious thing, dude," said Krusty trying not to break down laughing. "You're not gonna believe this. Nobody here knows what dope is."

"Bullshit."

"It's true, bro. I swear it."

"A whole building full of horticulturists who've never heard of one of the most popular plants in human history?"

"They're all fuckin' dweebs, bro. Every single person here is straight out of university and into some shitty government job. They only know what was in their textbooks."

"How does that explain why they're all smoking joints?"

"Svenson and I have been having a bit of fun. We've been getting people stoned all morning and telling them it's a new kind of medication that acts as a cough suppressant."

"And they believe that?"

"Totally, bro. It's a crack up."

JJ shook his head and looked over to realise that the door to Bennings' room was open. He took a couple of steps in that direction and looked inside the room which was empty.

"Where's Bennings?" he asked Krusty.

"Dunno, dude. Haven't seen him this morning."

"Alright, this is bad. We gotta get this place cleaned up before Bennings sees it. C'mon."

They walked back into the room and JJ started going from person to person and politely asking them to leave. This turned out not to be so easy as many of the people were in a stoned state where getting them to understand a request took work and then getting them to actually move once they had understood took more work. He had cleared the room of all but the last three people who were as good as stuck to the seats around the card table and, in the case of Nakamura, getting violent about not wanting to leave when Bennings and Spiffo strode into the room.

"They're cheating, I tell you," said Bennings casting about for something and finally spotting a half smoked joint in the mouth of the German competitor who was sitting at the table.

"See, this is the stuff," he said pulling the joint out of the German's mouth and holding it up to Spiffo who sniffed at it a few times.

"What's it supposed to be?" asked Spiffo.

"I'm not sure. But I think it's what they've been using to get these absurd results. Kale can't grow like that," he said pointing to the row of kale. "It's not possible without the use of some kind of stimulant. I think this is stimulant."

Spiffo turned to JJ and held up the joint.

"Do you want to tell me what this is or shall I send it off to the lab to get them to tell me?"

"It's a, ummm, it's..."

JJ was racking his brain for a plausible excuse and the only thing he could think of was what Krusty had just told him.

"It's a brand new medication we've been working on. It acts as a cough suppressant."

As if to prove JJ's point, the German at the table let out a throaty, THC-inspired cough that crackled like a boot stomping on a piece of bubble wrap.

"Doesn't look like it works," said Spiffo.

"That's because you removed the medicine before it had a chance to take effect," said JJ stepping forward and taking the joint from Spiffo and placing it back in the German's mouth. "He needs the full dose."

The German took a long toke and gave a cheesy, stoned smile as he exhaled in the direction of Spiffo.

"See, it works," said JJ. "No more coughing."

"This doesn't make sense," said Bennings suspiciously. "There's been people coughing in here all morning."

"Imagine how much more they'd be coughing if they weren't using the cough suppressant, dude," said Krusty.

Spiffo didn't look particularly convinced but he also wasn't prepared to push the matter any further.

"Look, we can't have any coughing during the taste test later. Do you understand? As I've already explained, the members of The Global Council have a zero tolerance policy on this matter. So, do whatever you've got to do, cough suppressants or whatever, and just make damn sure there's no coughing later. Am I understood?"

"Yes, sir," said JJ.

"And clean this place up. You've got beer bottles and whisky bottles everywhere. What is this? You're supposed to be professionals."

"Sorry, sir. We got a little carried away with the celebrations since it looks like we're going to win the competition."

Spiffo gave a "hmmmph" before marching out of the room followed by a bitter-looking Bennings.

"I can't believe that worked," said JJ slumping down on a seat near the table.

"Dweebs, dude. They're all dweebs," said Krusty pulling out a bag of weed. "Now, if you don't mind, the doctor says I need to take some more cough medicine."

***

There had been a good couple of hours of peace and quiet, if you didn't count the loud snoring that came from the other end of the room where Krusty and Svenson had finally crashed out on the mattresses provided by Mrs Lovechild. After cleaning up the area, moving the bottles of booze over to the corner, clearing away cards and poker chips and gathering up the numerous half-smoked and sometimes unsmoked joints that were lying around everywhere, JJ sat at the round table reflecting on the absurdity of the situation. He couldn't figure out which part was the most crazy; the fact that there was sewage getting pumped through the hydroponics system in front of him but nobody among the competition, including Bennings, had deduced from the smell that this was driving the spectacular results achieved by Svenson's kale or the fact that you could a wave a lit joint under the nose of these people and they didn't know what it was. It was almost as if they weren't even making use of their senses, or their brains. The lack of curiosity was all the more strange given that the discovery of any of these things would have led to Team Melbourne getting disqualified which was in the interests of every other team in the competition.

And so, despite all the odds, they were about to win the competition. But winning the competition was only the start of the problems. With the news that his every move was under surveillance from the Corporation, JJ faced a choice between breaking his promise to Snake not to see Amber or breaking his promise to Amber that they would meet that afternoon and he would tell her everything. After turning the matter over in his mind, he decided to break his promise to Amber on the assumption that at least she wouldn't have his legs broken or tie a rock around his legs and throw him in the harbour. Although, there might be an off-chance she would get Cody to do it for her. In any case, his best bet was to go through the motions required with the ridiculous white spray bottle the following day and thereby discharge his duty to the Corporation. Snake couldn't hold anything against him after that and he could see Amber without fear of reprisal.

Amber was sure to be disappointed but he figured he could make it up to her. In a weird way, they had bonded over the whole Todhammerstein question the previous night and he knew he could tell her the truth and she would forgive him. What would happen after that was anybody's guess. He couldn't exactly stay in Sydney and pretend to be Paul Wochensky indefinitely. On the other hand, the idea of asking Amber to come back to Tittybong with him and running the town money supply on behalf of Macbeth didn't appeal to him either. Perhaps they could run away together. Somewhere new. Maybe up north to Queensland.

JJ's daydreams of escape were broken when one of the officials knocked on the door and announced that the final taste test ceremony was fifteen minutes away and he should prepare his three best kale leaves. He decided to let Svenson and Krusty continue sleeping down the end of the room since their participation in the ceremony was not required. He wandered among the kale plants looking for the best leaves but, like the dope plants in Svenson's factory, they all looked the same so chose three at random, placed them into the plastic container, straightened out his clothing and his hair, put on the face mask required to be worn in front of the Global Council members and walked out the door.

In the hall, everything had been set up exactly as it had for the previous day's test. There were the three tables in the middle where the judges would sit while a queue for the servers had already formed. JJ took his place at the end of the line and received a crooked glance from Bennings who was halfway along. JJ noticed that several other members of the queue were looking a bit zonked out no doubt still feeling the effects of Krusty's Special. Nakamura in particular, who was right in front of JJ, was gently swaying from one side to the other in a kind of daydream.

After a couple of minutes, Spiffo, Johansson and the three judges arrived with Spiffo once again taking on the role of master of ceremonies. The three judges looked almost identical to the ones from the previous day; two men and one woman in late middle age, overweight with ruddy complexions. Whatever these people were eating in their day-to-day lives, kale was probably not high on the list. It reminded JJ that most of this was just for show; a piece of political theatre complete with stages props and costumes in the form of face coverings. Spiffo read his lines, something about innovation being at the heart of the Global Council's new initiatives blah, blah, blah. The judges placed their napkins over their laps and the show began.

First up was Argentina who received some light praise. Botswana fared better. Chile not so good. On it went until they got to the German whose joint Spiffo had inspected earlier at the poker table. Like Nakamura, he looked a little worse for wear but managed, with an amount of clumsiness, to get a kale leaf onto each judge's plate before stepping off to the side to await the verdict. There was complete silence in the basement, a room that was essentially one giant echo chamber featuring concrete walls, concrete floor and concrete ceiling that reverberated the slightest sound. It was into this echo chamber that the German coughed. It was much like the cough from earlier at the poker table although this time it sounded less like a boot stomping on bubble wrap and more like a cowboy cracking a whip inside Satan's bong chamber. It was the kind of cough that would have impressed even a hardened smoker like Krusty if the circumstances were different. But these circumstances were not conducive to a cough. Not at all. The volume seemed magnified by the room as it bounced off walls, floor and ceiling. The judges responded as if it had been a gun shot. They recoiled in shock and when the German let out a second, throatier cough, they leapt out of their seats with an agility that belied their age.

When Snake had said that the Global Council members were germaphobes, he wasn't lying. JJ saw it now with his own eyes. The judges had a complete meltdown. They called on Spiffo to do something and his response was based less on irrational fear and more on fear for his political aspirations. Like a rabbit surrounded by a pack of foxes, his eyes darted around as if looking for a means of escape. He caught sight of JJ and came rushing over with a mad look in his eye.

"The cough medicine, Wochensky. Get me some cough medicine," he whispered furiously.

"What?" said JJ who in the heat of the moment had forgotten all about the earlier incident.

"The smokable medicine," said Spiffo placing his hand to his mouth miming the smoking of a cigarette.

Finally, JJ twigged. He ran back into the room and found the place where he had hidden the joints he'd collected earlier. Not knowing how many he would need, he simply grabbed the whole stack and rushed back handing them to Spiffo who ran over to the judges as if he was carrying a defibrillator to a heart attack victim.

"Your excellencies, I'm terribly sorry for this dangerous exposure incident. I hold here in my hand the latest technology in protective medication developed right here in Australia. I encourage you take it right now. It will protect against the coughing you have been exposed to."

The judges seemed eager to take Spiffo up on the offer. They grabbed a joint each but apparently had no idea what to do with it. Spiffo also had no clue.

"Wochensky," he shouted.

JJ realised what he needed to do. He ran back into the room and grabbed a lighter off the poker table before sprinting back to where the judges were.

"You need to smoke it," he said taking a joint and holding it up to his mouth to demonstrate the technique.

Once his joint was lit. He held the lighter up to the first judge who tentatively leaned into it with the joint Spiffo had given her. She took a drag and immediately began coughing.

"Don't worry, that's all part of it," said JJ. "That's good. That shows that it's working."

The judge seemed to accept this explanation and went back for a second drag which she executed with more competence inhaling properly and exhaling a stream of smoke. JJ moved to the second judge who seemed to be more of a natural taking a strong drag the first time. The third judge held the joint up to the flame but nothing happened.

"You have to suck on the end," said JJ.

Still nothing happened.

"Inhale," said JJ.

Still nothing.

Finally, JJ took the joint from the judges mouth and inserted the one he had already lit in its place. The judge finally got the hang of it and took a deep toke.

JJ stood back and watched the spectacle of three late middle aged people smoking weed for the first time. It was, ironically, almost certainly the best medicine for the problem which beset them. Their anxiety quickly gave way to a feeling of mild euphoria. Smiles broke out and then even some giggling from the female judge who realised this was not in keeping with the gravity of the occasion and tried to suppress it which only made the giggling worse. After about a minute or so of this and with the judges clearly having calmed down, Spiffo looked on with equal measures of surprise and relief.

"How are your excellencies feeling?" he asked.

"Wonderful," came the reply. "Kudos for a rapid response, Mr Spiffo. We owe you a debt of gratitude."

"Are you excellencies ready to recommence with the taste testing?" asked Spiffo.

Their excellencies did not immediately answer him on account of a new outbreak of giggling.

"Your excellencies?" repeated Spiffo.

"Yes, yes, let's get it over with it," said the third judge in a moment of dope-induced candour.

Spiffo gave JJ a wave to indicate that he should return to his position. The German competitor was still waiting off to the side. His kale leaves were still on the plates. The judges did not bother with either their napkins or their cutlery but picked up the leaf and shovelled it into their mouths in one go.

"Mmmmm," said the third judge. "This is outstanding."

"Excellent," said the second. "This is a flavour I've never tasted before."

"More," said the third judge waving to the next competitor in the line who stepped forward and had barely placed a leaf on the plate of each judge when it was greedily scooped up and eaten.

"Keep 'em coming. I'm starving all of a sudden", said the first judge as the next competitor deposited their leaf followed by the next and what was supposed to be a taste test was quickly becoming a speed test to see how much kale could be consumed in the quickest possible time.

They continued down the line through Bennings who was rebuked for wasting the judges time by taking a bow. He plonked the kale down on their plates and skulked off towards his teammates who appeared horrified by the scene unfolding before them.

Finally it came to JJ who opened the plastic container and pulled out three giant leaves that were at least three times bigger than any other leaf that had been served so far not to mention greener and more lush by far.

"That's more like it," exclaimed the first judge who held the leaf up briefly to appreciate its size before proceeding to stuff the whole thing in her mouth and began chewing like her life depended on it.

"All kale should be this big," announced the second.

"Mmmmwoooaarr," cried the third.

What he was really trying to say, although his mouth was full of kale, was "more!" which is exactly what he did say once he'd finished chewing.

"More!"

JJ didn't need to be told twice. He sprinted back to the room and began ripping as many leaves as he could off the plants. Once he had as much as he could carry, he ran back to the table and dumped them on the judges plates who began greedily stuffing their faces. This went on for three rounds before the judges, possibly now suffering from munchies regret, finally sat back and decided they'd had enough.

"Mr Spiffo, I think we have a winner," announced the first judge gesturing towards JJ.

Johansson, who had been keeping himself inconspicuous the whole time, suddenly stepped forward.

"Congratulations to our champions, Team Melbourne," he announced holding JJ's arm up in the air.

"Hang on, we haven't calculated the yield yet," objected Spiffo.

"Do we need to bother?" asked Johansson holding up one of the giant leaves that was left on one judge's plate.

"No, I guess not," said a crestfallen Spiffo.

"A round of applause for our winners," said Johansson and those assembled began clapping.

With the final taste test over, the judges were escorted out by Johansson who did not miss the opportunity to remind them that the team they had awarded victory to was his team. Spiffo followed along behind with a grumpy expression. JJ, still in a state of incomprehension at what had just happened, wandered back to the room, closed the door and lay down on the mattress to finally get some rest for himself.

***

It was just past nine o'clock in the evening and JJ was already wondering how he was going to keep himself awake as he sat in the empty room of Team Melbourne with nothing for company except a long row of kale plants. Even though they had technically won the competition, Todhammerstein was due to tour the room the next day and Johansson wanted to make absolutely sure there were no last minute shenanigans from Bennings. Krusty and Svenson had offered to stay and keep him company but he liked the idea of having time alone. There were many things to think through. But the thinking hadn't helped much. He still had no clear answer or direction, no pathway out of the predicament other than to go through with ceremony tomorrow and see what happened afterwards.

Earlier in the afternoon, he'd sent Amber a message saying he couldn't meet that evening as planned but they could definitely get together the following afternoon. She hadn't replied and so he'd sent more messages and finally even tried to call her but with no luck. No doubt she was pissed off. From her point of view, it was one more lie; one more broken promise. In a way, though, it was good. It was one less thing to worry about. He could focus on the goal which was to get through whatever was going to happen the next day. He looked down at the small white spray bottle on the card table and tried to run through in his mind once again the different scenarios about how it might go, what excuses he could try to make so that it didn't look like a set up and what might happen afterwards if things went wrong. And then his phone beeped. He pulled it out to check the message. It was from Amber.

I'm outside. Can you let me in?

Outside where?

The building at 12 Alice Street. I'm standing next to door that leads to the basement.

JJ immediately suspected foul play. How could Amber know he was here? And how would she know where the building was? And how did she know that he would be in the basement? And how would she know there was a door to the basement? It was true that she could have gotten this information from her father, so he couldn't rule out that it really was her. But he had the strong suspicion that it was a setup, although who would be behind it? Snake? Was this a test of loyalty? And, if so, how did they get Amber's phone?

A second problem was McCutcheon. He was on night shift again and JJ had said hello to him earlier in the evening before pretending to be tired and retiring to the room so he didn't have to talk to him. Nevertheless, McCutcheon would be around and if he caught JJ and Amber together he would tell Snake and that would open a whole other can of worms.

JJ got up and opened the door to the room to see if anybody was around. The hall area was empty. There were no other competitors in the rooms. He'd already checked that. The idea of just ignoring Amber's message occurred to him. He could make up an excuse the next day about how he hadn't seen the message or had a flat battery or whatever. This seemed the best move. Even if it was Amber outside, it was better not to see her now.

No sooner had he decided on that path of action when three loud thumps emanated from the door at the other end of the hall. The sound ricocheted through the space like a hammer. JJ realised his hand was forced. The noise would attract McCutcheon and that would be the worst possible scenario. He skipped over to the door casting a glance up the stairs on the way to make sure McCutcheon wasn't coming down.

"Hi, Jay," said Amber giving a friendly wave as JJ opened the door.

The friendliness of her demeanour was offset by the sinister look of the three large men standing on the steps behind her. Front and centre was none other than Cody dressed in the same leather vest from the previous night. JJ recognised the two others from the table in the nightclub.

"How did you know I was here?" he whispered to Amber.

"I asked Dad."

"Ok. So, what's up?"

"Cody needs access to the building. Just for five minutes."

"Why?"

"None of your business," snapped Cody from behind.

"It's not a big deal," continued Amber. "He and the boys just want to install a few cameras. That's all. They'll be really quick."

"What do you need cameras for?"

"Why does anybody need cameras. To see with," said Cody.

"And what are you hoping to see?" said JJ addressing Cody for the first time.

"A certain man whose name starts with Tod and ends in Stein."

"I've already told you that's not a good idea. Things are already underway to take care of that situation. Your plan will just screw everything up."

"What? You're gonna take out Todhammerstein now?"

"Yes. That's exactly what I'm going to do."

Cody laughed.

"Bullshit. You're just making shit up so we'll go away. Well, we're not going anywhere, Mr North Shore. We can do this the easy way or the hard way. The choice is yours."

The two goons behind Cody took a step forward into positions where it was clear that JJ was not going to be able to escape back into the basement.

"It'll only take a few minutes," said Amber putting her hand on JJ's forearm.

JJ realised he had no choice.

"Fine. But there's a security guard around here so let me check to make sure he's not around. Ok?"

Cody gave a nod to one of the others who jumped down from the stairs and stood right behind JJ to ensure he couldn't close the door behind him as he walked back inside.

"I'll hold the door for you, sweetheart," he said in JJ's ear.

JJ stuck his head back into the basement to see that the coast was clear. It was. He gave a nod to the guy behind who pulled the door open fully and they entered the hall of the basement. JJ walked over and took up a position at the bottom of the stairs to keep a lookout for McCutcheon while Cody and the two goons moved with a speed and efficiency that signalled that they had done this kind of work before. They'd brought step ladders with them which enabled them to place the cameras up near the ceilings on the relatively low walls of the basement.

True to their word, Cody and the two others were finished within minutes and they exited out of the basement door with JJ following along to make sure they were gone.

"You guys go along without me," said Amber. "I'll meet up with you tomorrow."

Cody and the others disappeared into the darkness and Amber turned around to face JJ.

"I was, umm, I was thinking maybe I could spend the night here," she said with a sultry smile.

"After you just held me to ransom?" said JJ.

"What? That? That's nothing. We're on the same team. We just have different ideas about how to get the result. You said yourself that you wanted to take out Todhammerstein. Besides, it's not like you haven't been lying to me the last few days is it? Now we're even."

JJ didn't know what to say.

"You're alone aren't you?" asked Amber.

"Yeah," said JJ.

"Well, let me keep you company."

Amber again pressed her body close to JJ's and again he didn't need much more convincing. He ushered her inside and quietly closed the door behind them.

Chapter 6

JJ's phone woke him again but this time it was the alarm clock. He'd set it for 8am, a trade-off between trying to get some kind of sleep and having time to work through all the issues that still needed to be worked through. Thankfully, one issue had been removed from the equation and that was Amber, although to put it in such utilitarian terms was to do a grave injustice to the pathos (and Eros) of the events of the preceding evening which had spilled over into the early hours of the morning.

Once they were along in the Team Melbourne room, there was no longer any reason not to do what JJ had promised: tell Amber everything. And that's what he had done, the full story from go to woah, the whole crazy tale beginning with a simple desire to let Phoebe buy a second hand mobile phone and ending, well, ending in the arms of a beautiful woman in a room full of giant kale plants that were being fertilised by human excrement (he'd left the excrement part out of it telling Amber the official story that the smell was due to an unresolved plumbing issue). He introduced Amber to the inner machinations of the country's greatest mafia don including the fact that "he" was a twelve year old girl. She heard about their crazy plan to make the most powerful man in the world catch a cold and thereby to bring down his empire without firing a shot. She heard about the ins and outs of the kale growing competition including the victory awarded by a bunch of stoned judges. And she heard of the final task that remained which was to spray Todhammerstein with the white bottle at the award ceremony the following day including the very likely possibility that this was just a ruse for some ulterior plan that Snake might have.

More importantly, Amber understood that JJ had only taken the mission so that he could warn her about the danger to her father; that he could easily have stayed back in Tittybong counting his money. He also finally admitted, as much to himself as to her, that he took the mission so he could have one more chance with her. Her heart melted when he told how he'd spent almost a whole month lying on the couch after she'd left. She kissed him on the cheek many times and apologised saying that she never wanted to leave but the seemingly definitive choice between city and town forced her hand and that she hated what had happened to the country and the man who was forcing it to happen; that she would do anything to stop it including helping JJ with the mission.

They began working through the details which JJ had already run over so many times in his mind. There were still many unknowns. Was the whole plan by Macbeth just a ruse? What was it a ruse for? How could Macbeth win the levers of power of the Australian government if she was able to take out Todhammerstein and what sort of assets and institutional structure did Macbeth have in the city to achieve that outcome. They talked about Cody and the goons from the nightclub and what they were doing with their cameras (Amber didn't know but they agreed it was safer to leave them in place). They talked a little about her father and what he could do to help. Eventually, it got late and with no resolution in sight they realised they'd be better off getting some sleep and tackling the issue with fresh eyes in the morning. That was not, to be sure, the only reason to stop the talking and let another, more pleasurable, form of communication take place before gathering a few hours of much needed rest before the big day.

And so once again JJ awoke with Amber in his arms and took a minute to savour the smell of her hair and the touch of her skin before allowing the worries of the world to intrude. He rolled over onto his back and looked up at the concrete ceiling above with its complex patterns of pipework, electrical wiring, circuit boxes, HVAC equipment and all the other accoutrements of the basement of a modern office building. He turned his head to the sewage pipes several metres away from where the bed was in the back corner of the room and it suddenly occurred to him that the shit and the piss that had powered Team Melbourne to success had all come from the upper levels of the building. The most powerful people in the country and even the world had fuelled their victory, so to speak. It was possible that Todhammerstein himself had made a deposit into the plumbing network that had ended up in the kale that he would eat in just a few hours. It was the cycle of life; the wheel of history; and today could be the day that the wheel turned for the better. Or maybe it would be just like Krusty said: eating shit.

Amber, who had also woken with the sound of the alarm, roused herself and slowly turned over to face JJ.

"Morning," she said placing her hand on his chest.

"Morning," he answered absently as if deep in thought.

"Come up with a solution yet?"

"Yeah. I think we should run away."

"Run away?"

"We get up, put on our clothes and just leave town."

"Where would we go? And how would we get out?"

"Don't you know anybody? Another canoeist perhaps?"

"It'd take a long time to canoe our way anywhere safe. Besides, what about Krusty and that other guy on your team?"

"Svenson."

"Yeah, you can't just leave Krusty and Svenson behind."

"I know," sighed JJ. "I'm not being serious. But it would be nice to just make all this go away."

"Have you thought about what you want to do?"

"Not seriously."

"Well, let's go through it from where we finished off last night."

"I remember where we finished off," said JJ with a cheeky smile.

"I mean before that," said Amber giving him a playful slap on the chest.

"Before that. Right. Well, there's two options to choose from. Either we go to your father first thing this morning, right now, and tell him everything. Or, we go through with the ceremony with Todhammerstein and see what comes of that."

"Right. And the pros of going to my father first are that we can ask him to provide you and the others with protection against Macbeth while also allowing him to take whatever measures he might think up."

"How do you think your father would take it? I mean, the whole idea of wiping out Todhammerstein?"

"I honestly don't know. My father and I are not exactly close. We live in the same house but we might as well be living in different countries. He's never home and when he is home he's always just running out the door."

"There's a chance that if we tell him the truth he's not gonna like it. Maybe he supports the Global Council. Plus, I'm pretty sure I've broken a whole lot of laws in the past few days not to mention the fact that I deceived him and lied to his face several times. He's got plenty of reason to be pissed with me. On top of all that, I'm officially a member of the biggest mafia organisation in the country. That's a whole lot of reasons for him not to want to help. He might just put me in jail and throw away the key."

"He would never do that!"

"Are you sure?"

Amber sighed.

"No. I'm not sure."

"So, that's one problem with the tell-your-dad idea. And the second problem is that if we tell him then nothing changes. Todhammerstein gets away scot free, the city walls stay closed, Macbeth takes over the country towns and everything goes to hell."

"So, you wanna go ahead with the ceremony?"

"Not really."

"What's the problem?"

"The problem is it's a stupid idea. Trying to infect somebody with a cold. It's crazy."

"It's not so stupid, you know. As you saw yesterday, the Global Council are massive hypochondriacs and germaphobes. I know that from experience too. Dad dragged me along to some functions run by the Council and it was a nuthouse. We always had to wear masks. For one of them, I had to wear a full hazmat suit."

"Just because they're germaphobes doesn't mean the plan will work. I mean, who's gonna catch a cold in the middle of summer?"

"You don't understand, these people have shielded themselves away from all germs their whole life. I don't know for sure, but it could be that they have no natural immunity. In that case, they would be highly susceptible to a cold virus."

"Even allowing that the idea could work, I have no idea what's in the plastic bottle and

I don't trust Snake and I don't trust Macbeth. They're mafia after all. I still think the most likely explanation is that the spray bottle thing is just a ruse for something else they wanna try."

"But that's not necessarily a bad thing. I mean, if the other idea works, whatever it is, we still get rid of Todhammerstein."

"And then your father is the next target."

"He's always going to be a target as long as people like Macbeth are around. There's nothing much we can do about that."

"We can warn him."

"Yeah, but we can do that after the ceremony."

There was a silence for a few seconds while they both thought about it some more. Finally, JJ spoke.

"Well, it sounds we have our answer. We go through with the ceremony and lets the chips fall where they may. That also has the added benefit of me fulfilling my obligations to Macbeth so they won't come after me. After it's done, we go and tell your father the truth. Then you and I escape to a tropical island."

"I like the sound of that," said Amber as she leaned in to kiss JJ.

While they were kissing, the door of the room opened and two pair of footsteps made their way towards the bed unrecognised. A familiar voice rang out:

"Morning, JJ. Morning, Amber. Long time, no see."

Amber, still naked from the night before, pulled the bed sheet up to her chin and turned to see Krusty and Svenson standing there holding some containers of take away food and coffee.

"Hi, Krusty," said Amber a little peevishly. "I see you've moved your operations to the city," she said gesturing to the hydroponics set up.

"Just spreading the love, baby. By the way, this is Svenson. Svenson this is Amber."

Svenson gave a small bow in Amber's direction.

"Now, we bought some food for JJ but we didn't know he'd have company so you'll have to share his portion between the two of you."

Krusty placed a muffin, a coffee and another item on the floor next to the bed.

"You all set for your big day, bro?"

"I think so," said JJ.

"Y'know, we were thinking, this is a lot like the start of World War One. Y'know how that terrorist killed that Duke somewhere. Archduke Todhammerstein's in for a bad day."

"Couldn't you find a more uplifting historical example than a war where tens of millions of people died?"

"Nah, that's the best we could think of. Enjoy your breakfast in bed, sweethearts."

***

It was almost time.

JJ had expected to be nervous but a strange kind of calm and self-assuredness had come over him as can often happen when the magnitude of an occasion overwhelms the mind's ability to fathom it. In this case it wasn't just the magnitude but the absurdity of the situation which prevented comprehension. He was about to stand in front of the most powerful person in the world and spray a bottle of what was probably water in front of him. If you'd told him two weeks' ago that this was the future that awaited him, JJ would have written you off as a madman and yet here he was sitting in the Team Melbourne room awaiting his fate.

Spiffo had come in earlier to explain how the ceremony would go. JJ, Krusty and Svenson were to stand at the front of the room beside the first container of kale. They were to wear two face masks which was the standard protocol around Todhammerstein. They were not to say or do anything other than what they were instructed to do. This was not a mere ceremonial formality. Todhammerstein never went anywhere with a crack squad of his most loyal and highly trained security personnel. They were armed to the teeth and instructed to shoot first and ask questions later if in the slightest doubt as to the safety of their boss. Unexpected movements could prove lethal.

Todhammerstein would be shown around the room for a bit by Johansson. JJ, Krusty and Svenson would then be presented to him as the winners of the competition and would receive their prize. Todhammerstein would be asked if he would like to sample the winning kale. If he agreed, JJ was to take the plate and tongs that were placed on a table nearby and present a single leaf to Todhammerstein. JJ should wait to receive the plate and that would be all.

JJ knew his window of opportunity to execute the spraying was in the handing of the plate to Todhammerstein. But the stakes had now been raised significantly by the addition of the armed guards to the equation. He didn't much like the idea of getting shot. He wondered whether he could just back out; play his role in the ceremony and skip the spraying part. How would Snake and Macbeth ever know that he hadn't done what was required? But that possibility was extinguished when he caught sight of McCutcheon loitering by the door listening in to Spiffo's address. No doubt McCutcheon would be watching the ceremony. If JJ didn't do what was required, McCutcheon would tell Snake and Snake would tell Macbeth. Thus, JJ had a choice of potentially being shot by Todhammerstein's guards or potentially being shot by Macbeth associates. In a way, it was this fact which calmed JJ down. He had no real choice and so there wasn't any point in worrying anymore. He would do what was necessary and let the chips fall where they may.

JJ was sitting with Amber and Svenson at the round table when Krusty came barging through the door.

"They're here, dudes!"

Krusty had been posted to the outside of the building to give maximum advance notice for the arrival of the honoured guests. Amber, who decided she'd like to be present for the ceremony, planned to casually intercept her father somewhere in the building and then use her status as daughter of the Prime Minister to get access.

"Good luck," she said grabbing JJ by both hands giving him a quick kiss.

"He's gonna need it," quipped Krusty as Amber gave him a slap on the arm on the way past as she walked out the door and headed for the foyer to put her plan into action.

"Take your positions!" shouted one of the officials as he stuck his head through the door of the room. "The ceremony is about to commence."

JJ, Krusty and Svenson began putting on their face masks while Bennings and Team Sydney and the German team, who were the second and third place getters in the competition, entered the room and took up their allotted position near the wall. It was hard to tell due to the mask over his mouth and nose, but JJ detected a look of malicious intent in Bennings' eyes although perhaps it was just ill will due to the fact that he would have to watch JJ collect the prize that Bennings coveted so much.

With masks secure, JJ, Krusty and Svenson took up their allocated spot just in time for the cavalry to arrive or, rather, the foot soldiers. Todhammerstein's personal guard was dressed as if they were going into battle against an army of killer robots. They were covered head to toe in full body armour while the black masks covering their mouths giving them the vague appearance of a team of ninjas. There were about fifteen altogether and they took up a variety of positions around the room. Each one had a machine gun slung around their shoulder as well as various other armaments signalling that any one of them could kill you five different ways before you'd even hit the floor.

From outside the room JJ could hear the familiar sound of Spiffo bloviating about the facility and the competition. Outside the door there appeared a group of people who looked to be media personnel including photographers and video cameramen and journalists. They began to funnel into the room and take up positions in a space that had been pre-assigned to them just opposite JJ against the wall where they would have a good angle for their photographs. It occurred to JJ that his, Krusty and Svenson's pictures were about to broadcast around the world including down to Melbourne where presumably friends, colleagues and family members of the real Wochensky, Blomfeld and Winfield would notice that they were imposters. No doubt at least one of them would alert the authorities. Starting that afternoon they would be wanted men, although it was JJ's hope that Johansson would be able to protect them at least from the official authorities. That is, of course, if he was sympathetic to their cause which could not be taken for granted. JJ started to wonder whether he wouldn't be better off seeking help from Macbeth instead but there was no time to think about it now. The show was about to begin.

JJ had never seen a picture of Todhammerstein and yet somehow he looked exactly as he'd imagined: elderly, wrinkled and a little stooped over. Aged in his early 80s, he was almost completely bald and was dressed in a black suit and bowtie. He was the only one in the room without a mask on with the exception of the person at his side who appeared to be his assistant, a young man who, JJ realised, was an albino. He was short and skinny with white hair and white eyes that he didn't mind accentuating with an all-white suit of the highest quality.

The assistant stood on the right hand side of Todhammerstein. On the left were Johansson and Spiffo who were masked for the first time that week signifying the increased protocols required when dealing with the big boss. Johansson was nearest and was now leading this part of the tour explaining some things about the layout of the room. As they entered, Spiffo peeled off and took up a place not far from the door standing in front of Bennings. Lastly came Amber who was now also masked. She gave JJ a wink as she took the spot next to Spiffo.

"And so we come to the final stop on the tour," explained Johansson as he led Todhammerstein into the room. "For the last four days we have been running our horticultural competition according to the rules specified by the Global Council. We have had teams from all around the world competing in this year's theme which I understand is also your personal favourite vegetable, Mr Todhammerstein, the ancient plant of kale which has been given a high-tech upgrade courtesy of our first class hydroponics setup. Each team was given identical apparatus creating a level playing field where the only variables to be tweaked were the nutrient and water inputs. In accordance with the Global Council's desire to increase kale yields by twenty percent according to the most recent five year plan, it was hoped the contest which has pitted the world's best horticulturists against each other would be able to help toward the fulfilment of that goal. I'm delighted to announce that the winners of the competition are an Australian team from the city of Melbourne who have, as you can see with your own eyes, surpassed all expectations. The yield increase here is an extraordinary two hundred and ninety-three percent over the global average kale yield for the last calendar year. But best of all is the taste which we will shortly give you the opportunity to experience for yourself. For now, allow me to introduce the winning contestants. We have here Paul Wochensky, Harold Blomfeld and the man who is the creator of the famous Winfield Method that has brought about these incredible results, Arnold Winfield."

JJ and the others stood perfectly still having been instructed not to shake hands or initiate any other gesture. Todhammerstein looked at them with his cold grey eyes that showed no particular emotion. JJ realised he was even uglier up close as his right eyelid hung lower than his left and his face was covered with things that were not quite scars, not quite pimples but more like discolourations as if someone has spilled ink on his face.

"Vat is ze secret formula to your method, Mr Vinfield?" asked Todhammerstein in a croak.

"It's a combination of things," answered Svenson, "but mostly to do with potassium sulphate."

"Lies!" came a shout from the door.

There was an audible gasp from the assembled crowd while more than a dozen machine guns swung in the direction of the source of the disruption which turned out to be a now terrified Bruce Benjamin Bennings who threw his hands up as if to signify "don't shoot". In one of his hands was a piece of paper.

"Errr, allow me to explain," he spluttered. "I have written evidence here that Team Melbourne did not make a single withdrawal from the nutrient store for the last two days of the competition. They have thereby broken the rules and must be disqualified."

Bennings waved the piece of paper in the air which was presumably the evidence of which he spoke but which was functioning more like a white flag that he hoped would spare him the wrath of the guards. Spiffo looked like he was about to speak, presumably to back up his man's claims, but Johansson in a voice of authority that JJ had not heard until now beat him to the punch.

"How dare you! Guards, remove this man from the room. The competition has been officially certified. We don't need to hear from any sore losers. You have brought the competition into disrepute."

Two of the guards grabbed Bennings by an arm each and practically carried him out of the room before he could say another word. Bennetson and Anderson followed them out and JJ caught sight of McCutcheon still loitering in the hall outside the door just outside the doorway.

"I'm terribly sorry, Your Excellency," said Johansson turning back to Todhammerstein. "As you can imagine, with the stakes in the competition so high it is understandable that there would be an element of friction among the competitors. I can assure you that was nothing more than sour grapes. Now, let us proceed. I think we are up to the awarding of the prizes."

Todhammerstein gave a nod to the assistant who held up a small black case. He opened it to reveal three shiny black plastic cards about the size of a credit card.

"His excellency, Herr von Todhammerstein, congratulates you on your victory," said the man in a pan European accent. "Your prize is an exclusive pass to tomorrow's Global Congress event. You are to have the great honour of sitting in the same bay as the members of the Global Council. Present this electronic ticket at the entrance point and you will be shown to your seats."

They each took the piece of plastic without saying anything or making any gesture as they had previously been instructed.

"And now, I would like to offer Your Excellency the chance to sample the winning kale," said Johansson.

"I vould," said Todhammerstein.

All of a sudden, JJ's heart began to thump in his chest as the peculiar feeling of equanimity deserted him. He felt like his feet had been dipped in giant vat of semi-dry concrete. He forced his left leg to raise and then twisted and stepped out with his right to pick up the plate and the tongs from the table that was right behind him. With more than a hundred eyes on him, many of which were in bodies whose hands were attached to machine guns, he tried to look professional, whatever that meant, in dislodging a single leaf from the rest of the nearest kale plant using the tongs and then placing it on the plate. With the job done he put the tongs down and took the single step back to his starting position. JJ caught sight of McCutcheon watching on intently from over Todhammerstein's left shoulder as if reminding him of his duty. He removed the spray bottle from his left pants pocket.

"If Your Excellency would like, I can add this kale condiment we have been working on in the lab," said JJ holding the bottle up to view. "Our scientific studies have shown that it improves the taste by thirty-seven percent."

JJ held his finger on the nozzle and looked into the grey eyes which seemed to register nothing at all but the head of Todhammerstein gave a nod. JJ held out the plate in front of him and placed the spray bottle directly behind so that it was pointing both at the plate and also at Todhammerstein. He pressed down as hard as he could on the nozzle. The burst of spray which came out couldn't have been more perfect. It was as if it knew what to do, beginning its journey en route to the kale but then defying gravity and turning upwards towards the face of its target. It was like an inverted mushroom cloud giving an uppercut to the jaw of the world's most powerful man. This was no mere metaphor, however, as Todhammerstein reacted exactly as if he had been punched, albeit in slow motion. He took a step back and to the left. Then, as if his legs were about to give way, he kind of twisted around like a sheet in the wind and then finally his head went back a few inches before hurling forward in what turned out to be a gigantic sneeze that saw his body fold in half like a piece of paper. At the exact moment that Todhammerstein's head flung forward a flash appeared from the doorway where McCutcheon stood holding a black handgun. The bullet, which would have hit Todhammerstein in the chest, instead blew straight into the side of the hydroponics container behind sending a stream of brown and yellow fluid shooting out onto the floor.

McCutcheon would not get a second chance. A volley of machine gun fire picked him up like a leaf in a gust of wind and blew him out the doorway. Amber and the others who were in the area threw themselves to the ground in terror but the firing ended as fast as it began and several guards ran out of the room to make sure the job was done. Several more formed a circle around Todhammerstein pushing JJ, Krusty and Svenson from the immediate vicinity so violently that it was all they could do to keep their footing. JJ regained his balance just in time to see Todhammerstein being escorted from the room inside a ring of guards who had guns drawn for any further action. Johansson, who had been at the centre of it all, stood there dumbfounded as if a tornado had gone past him on all sides. He took a step backwards from the growing pool of brown-yellow fluid that was gathering on the floor in front of him.

For some time, nobody knew what to do. Nobody, that is, except Spiffo. He sprung into action as if he had foreseen exactly this eventuality.

"Guards, arrest this man," he said pointing at Johansson. "And his daughter too."

Spiffo pointed to Amber who was still sitting on the floor in a defensive position.

"We have evidence of malfeasance in this competition and that is reason to believe these two are actively involved in this assassination attempt."

"Hang on a minute...," began Johansson but it was too late.

The guards jumped into action like robots. They grabbed Johansson and Amber and removed them from the room.

"Hey!" shouted JJ who tried to go over and help out but was prevented from doing so by the general pandemonium as all the media scurried for the door.

A couple of the guards also stepped into JJ's path making it clear that he wasn't to leave. Soon it was just JJ, Krusty and Svenson with the remaining guards and Spiffo. Bennings re-entered the room like a detective who had just solved a high profile case. He walked over to the puddle on the floor and squatted down to inspect it. His face scrunched up at the smell.

"Is this what I think it is?" he asked more to himself than anybody else.

Then a look of understanding spread across his face.

"Of course. That would explain the lack of nutrients."

"What have you found?" asked Spiffo shuffling across to take a look for himself.

"Do you wanna tell him?" asked Bennings giving JJ a sly grin.

JJ just stood there with his jaw clenched.

"It looks to me to be equal parts shit and piss," Bennings explained to Spiffo. "That would explain the nasty smell that's been hanging around here for the last few days.

"But it's coming out of the kale," observed Spiffo.

"Exactly. That's how Team Melbourne managed to fertilise their plants after we cut off their nutrient supply."

"So, you just tried to feed the leader of the world shit?" asked Spiffo addressing the three.

"It's more than he deserves," answered Svenson.

"Well, I'll be damned," said Spiffo who sounded rather upbeat about the situation.

"What does this mean?" asked Bennings.

"What does it mean?" said Spiffo suddenly smiling broadly. "It means I've got an open and shut case against Johansson who was the sponsor of Team Melbourne. It means I'm about to be the new Prime Minister of this country."

Spiffo was so excited by this idea that he started to almost skip out of the room.

"What about these three?" asked Bennings pointing to JJ, Krusty and Svenson.

Spiffo turned around in the doorway and thought about it for a couple of seconds.

"Lock them in here for now til we figure out what to do with them. Guards, mind the door. If anybody tries to enter or leave, shoot them."

With that Spiffo left the room and Bennings turned to JJ and the others.

"Well, I guess this means I'm the real winner of the competition," he smiled.

"Maybe. But you'll always be a loser," said Krusty.

"Tell that to the judge, mate. If you even get to see a judge, that is."

Bennings gave a smirk and held up his piece of paper as if proving his superiority before walking out. The guards also left. The door closed behind them and once again there was peace and quiet. And the smell of shit.

***

"Dude, we're getting hungry in here. You have to get us some food."

"What are you talking about, you've got half a tonne of kale. Healthiest food there is. You'll be in tip top shape in no time."

"Yeah, but I need to use the toilet."

"Just take a dump in your kale. Isn't that what you sickos have been doing for the last week?"

Krusty had been hammering away at the guard on the other side of the door for about fifteen minutes trying to find an excuse to leave the room. At first, the guard hadn't responded at all but he'd become quite chatty in the last few minutes and even seemed to be enjoying himself now. Krusty figured it was best to cut his losses. He gave a final thump on the door then walked back to the card table where Svenson was amusing himself by playing solitaire. JJ was lying on one of the mattresses a few metres away staring into space. Krusty had been unable to get a word out of him since the incident with Todhammerstein.

"Shame about McCutcheon," said Krusty sitting down at the table with Svenson. "He was a good dude."

"He was a kamikaze," said Svenson without looking up from his card game.

"I know. What a trip. He must have known the whole time that he was gonna get blown away and he still went through with it. Still, not a bad way to go out. He spent his last days drinking whisky, smoking dope and playing cards. I'd take that."

"He was an idiot," came a scratchy but fiery voice from the mattress to Krusty's right.

"Eh, you're awake, bro."

"Yes, I'm awake. Awake to the fact that we were betrayed; just pawns in Macbeth's little game."

"Yeah, but you knew that before we took the mission, dude. We knew they were probably lying. Check out this high-tech piece of gear."

Krusty grabbed the top of the white spray bottle that was on the table nearby and dangled it around in the air.

"I can't believe we fell for that shit," muttered JJ.

"We didn't fall for anything. We knew it was a ruse. If I remember correctly, the main reason you wanted to come was so you could save your girlfriend and her old man."

"And I failed miserably at that task too," said JJ lifting himself up off the mattress and stretching his legs. "This is pretty much the worst possible outcome. Todhammerstein's still there and now Spiffo is gonna use this incident to steal the Prime Ministership. God knows what they'll do with Amber and her father."

"God knows what they'll do with us, bro. Death by firing squad seems the most likely outcome at this point. Hey, isn't blood and bone a good fertiliser too, bro? Maybe they can feed us to the kale."

"Is this a time for joking?"

"Better to joke about it than whine about it."

"I'm not whining."

"Well, what are we gonna do? I've at least been trying with the guard at the door while you've been lying around moping again."

"We need to kill Todhammerstein," said JJ.

"I thought you didn't want to kill him?"

"I've changed my mind."

"Ok. But don't you want to save Amber and her father too?"

"Of course."

"Shouldn't we do that before killing Todhammerstein?"

"We can do both at the same time if they're together."

"I doubt they're together. I think we can be pretty sure Todhammerstein has been taken somewhere safe that's nowhere near Amber and her father."

"We need to find out where they are," said JJ. "And we need somebody with some muscle who can fight against those soldiers."

Krusty looked over at JJ who said the word they were both thinking.

"Macbeth."

"Exactly. And we're still part of the Corporation and the Corporation is supposed to help its members."

"Alright, bro. So, we know who to go to. Do we know where to go? I mean, we've never actually seen where the headquarters is."

"I've got Snake's phone number," said JJ pulling his phone out of his pocket and holding it up. "He said I can call him if we get into trouble. The real problem is how are we gonna get out of this room."

"Can we ask Snake to get us out?"

"Maybe. But even Macbeth might have trouble breaking in here. I mean, you'd have to bring a small army to fight against those soldiers. If we can get out first and then call for help that would improve our chances."

JJ and Krusty looked around at the concrete walls, the concrete ceiling and the concrete floor and drew the obvious conclusion that there was no way out. Then Svenson spoke without looking up from his card game.

"I can get us out."

JJ and Krusty both looked at him.

"What?"

"I can get us out," he repeated.

"So why the hell didn't you say something?"

Svenson shrugged.

"Show us how."

Svenson took a few moments to finish off his card game then got up and started walking to the back wall. JJ and Krusty followed him.

"This pipe," he said pointing to the sewage pipe which ran through the wall and had been disconnected from the pipe above so Svenson could run the sewage into the hydroponics system. "This pipe is not bolted down on the outside because I had to move it slightly when I was hooking the system up. We can push on this pipe and it will fall out of the wall and then we can climb out."

JJ and Krusty crouched down and squinted a little as if to verify the truth of what Svenson had said. It seemed plausible. The pipe was wide although its diameter was such that squeezing a human out of the hole that would be left in the wall might not be so easy. In any case, it was worth a shot.

"Use your foot and push on the count of three," said Svenson as he, JJ and Krusty stood in front of the pipe and placed a foot each on the end.

"One, two, three."

They each pushed and were surprised at how easily the pipe slid forward as if it was greased by some hidden lubricant. They tried again and now the end of the pipe was almost flush with the wall.

"This is our last chance," warned Svenson. "Make sure you put every bit of energy in so the pipe falls out of the wall completely."

"One, two, three."

There was a loud clang as the L-shaped pipe fell away from the wall and tipped over onto its side on the concrete outside. Svenson, with a display of agility that would have impressed a special forces commando, grabbed onto the water pipe that was directly above the newly created hole in the wall and swung his torso through the hole finishing off the manoeuvre with something resembling a game of limbo as he walked forward while keeping his body horizontal until he clear swung clear and stood upright outside. Krusty went next while JJ had the presence of mind to check the room for anything that was worth taking with them. The only thing he could find was the white spray bottle which was not of any practical use but he liked the idea of presenting it to Snake as a symbol of his deceit. He grabbed it off the table and ran back to find Krusty stuck in the wall at the midriff with half his body on the outside and the other half still inside. He clung desperately to the water pipe above.

"Dude, little help," he croaked.

"I'll grab the legs and you push from the other side, JJ," yelled Svenson from the outside.

"One, two, three."

JJ braced himself and pushed as hard as he could on Krusty's shoulders. Nothing moved.

"Hold your stomach in," JJ instructed.

"I am holding my stomach in, bro."

"One more time," yelled Svenson. "One, two, three."

This time there was movement and Svenson continued to pull and JJ continued to push until Krusty's midriff was clear and he was able to wriggle his upper body out of the hole. JJ, who was skinnier than both Svenson and Krusty, had the easiest time of all and was through the wall with no trouble.

"Let's get the hell out of here before somebody notices," he said and they ran across the road and into the park opposite.

***

Snake, it's JJ. We need somewhere to hide. Have escaped from 12 Alice Street and are in the park opposite

Hello, Mr JJ. Wait near the pergola. A black van will arrive within five minutes.

Snake wasn't lying.

Four minutes and twenty-eight seconds later the van pulled up and JJ, Krusty and Svenson hurried over and jumped into the back. A Macbeth associate handed them each the familiar blindfold to put on but it was only another four and a half minutes before they'd arrived at their destination which, they quickly realised, was Macbeth HQ. As JJ removed his blindfold and stepped out of the back of the van to see the familiar white painted concrete walls he realised that they must still be in Kirribilli. It seemed like a very strange location for the country's foremost mafia organisation.

"Well, well, you boys made it out safe," said Snake who was waiting outside the van.

"No thanks to you," said JJ. "Aren't you supposed to rescue us and stuff. Y'know, the Corporation taking care of its members and all that."

"Rescue missions take time to organise, Mr JJ. And, anyway, you're standing here now, aren't you? Safe and sound. Why don't you come over to the bar and have a drink and relax. You must be buzzing after all the excitement."

"If by *excitement* you mean watching McCutcheon get blown away, then, yes, we are *buzzing*."

"McCutcheon did his duty for the Corporation. It's just a shame that his mission was not successful."

"Yeah, and our mission was a fake," said JJ holding up the white spray bottle like a lawyer in a courtroom.

"You played your part and did it well. We couldn't have done it without you."

"Our mission was bullshit, though, wasn't it?"

"If I told you the truth, you wouldn't have done it properly."

"Well, we have another mission to achieve now and we need your help."

"Oh?"

"I need you to tell me where Spiffo is keeping Johansson and Amber."

"What makes you think I know that?"

"C'mon, Snake. You have eyes everywhere. Remember?"

"And if I tell you where they are, what are you going to do?"

"Try and save them."

"Then that's exactly why I'm not going to tell you. It's a suicide mission."

"You were happy to let McCutcheon go on a suicide mission."

"McCutcheon's mission served the purposes of the Corporation. Your mission serves no purpose."

"It does to me."

"Then you go and find them."

"I want to speak to Macbeth."

Snake broke out laughing.

"Mr JJ, you've gotten hysterical with all the excitement, haven't you. I think you need that drink. I'll make it a double shot."

Snake began to walk towards the bar.

"I have something to offer," said JJ. "Something Macbeth wants."

"What's that?"

"Our award for winning the competition. Todhammerstein gave us tickets to the Congress tomorrow. We'll be sitting in the same box as him and the other Global Council high flyers."

"Uh-uh," said Snake in a tone that signalled for JJ to continue.

"That means we have another chance to take out Todhammerstein. We are prepared to offer that chance to Macbeth and in return we ask for information about where to find Johansson and Amber and the opportunity to try and rescue them."

"Interesting, Mr JJ. Very interesting. You're getting pretty good at this."

"I'm learning from a pro."

"Alright. Go and wait in the bar and I'll see what I can do."

***

About thirty minutes later Snake returned to the bar where Krusty and Svenson were already into their third whisky. JJ had drunk a single to calm his nerves but otherwise wanted to remain sharp.

"Alright, gents, this way please," said Snake gesturing for them to follow as he led them back down a corridor that was identical to the others with white painted concrete walls interspersed by large metal doors at varying intervals.

At the end of the corridor they walked through an open doorway into a large cavernous concrete room. The area to the left was completely empty while over on the right wall there were a number of items of domestic furniture including a dressing table, a standalone wooden closet and a few baskets and other storage items. It looked a little bit like a girl's bedroom. In the middle of the room was another piece of furniture JJ recognised from his initiation ceremony. It was the throne and on the throne was the familiar face of a certain twelve year old girl her brown hair still done up in pigtails and her feet still dangling off the ground. She was dressed in a frilly dress with dainty black shoes rather like a princess except all in black.

JJ, Krusty and Svenson had taken only a few steps into the room when they were grabbed from behind and thrown to the ground in an almost perfect repeat of the manoeuvre from their initiation ceremony. Once again, their clothing was removed down to their underpants. JJ half expected to get pissed on again. But this time, there was a more logical purpose to the events. Several associates began to rifle through their pockets retrieving whatever they could find inside which amount to nothing more than a few wallets, a few mobile phones and a few bags of weed, lighters and cigarette papers from Krusty's pants. Once satisfied that they had searched the clothing, one of the associates turned to Macbeth.

"Shall we do a full cavity search?" he asked.

"A fully cavity what!?" shouted Krusty.

"What are you looking for?" said JJ. "Just ask and we'll tell you. We're associates of the Corporation, aren't we?"

"The passes to the Congress," said Snake. "Where are they?"

"Hah. I hid them somewhere you'll never find them," said JJ. "You didn't think I was dumb enough to bring them in here, did you?"

Snake thought about it for a second.

"You're getting a little too good at this game, Mr JJ. Alright, let them up."

The men relaxed their grip and JJ, Krusty and Svenson returned to their feet and began putting their clothes back on.

"Just once I'd like to be able to come here and keep my clothes on," said Krusty.

Once they had straightened themselves out they followed Snake over to a position about five metres in front of the throne.

"Well, if it isn't our newest members," said Macbeth in her high pitched but still adult-sounding tone of voice. "Come to blackmail me, have you?"

"We've come to make a deal," said JJ.

"Same thing. Ok, what's the deal?"

"You will tell me where I can find Johansson and Amber so that we can free them from whatever Spiffo has in mind for them. In addition, you will agree not to commit violence against either of them. Forever."

"And what do I get out of this?"

"I will go to the Global Council congress tomorrow and kill Todhammerstein."

"You? You couldn't kill a fly."

"Give me a gun and show me how to use it. I'll be within metres of him. How hard can it be?"

"Pffft, what sort of deal is this. I can just order you to go to the Congress. You are a member of the Corporation. It is your duty to do what I say."

"Nope. That's the other part of it. We are no longer members of the Corporation. Once the deal is done, we're out."

"Not yet you're not. I can still order you to do the job."

"Then I'll refuse. And you won't get your chance to be rid of Todhammerstein."

"I'll have you tortured."

"C'mon, dude. Why do you want control of the whole country anyway?" asked Krusty.

Macbeth seemed taken aback as if nobody had ever asked her that kind of question before.

"Because I do."

"Because why?"

"Because I like having total power. It makes me feel good."

"Wouldn't you rather share, bro?"

"Total power is not a good idea," added Svenson. "Too much work and too much cognitive load for a single person. Plus, political history shows that power taken by violence can only be maintained by violence which inevitably ends up recoiling on the initiator like a rubber band of death and destruction."

"Yeah, what he said. It's better to share the power, bro."

"I don't like sharing."

"You've got a heap of power with the Corporation. Let the politicians run the country. It's a boring job anyway."

Snake walked over and began whispering in Macbeth's ear. She whispered back in turn. After about thirty seconds of this, he stepped back and Macbeth made an announcement.

"Alright, I accept your offer. You take out Todhammerstein and I agree to leave Johansson and his daughter alone. Since he is no longer Prime Minister, I have no use for him anyway."

"What do you mean?" asked JJ.

"Spiffo is the new Prime Minister and, as it happens, he and Johansson are located in the same place. I will send men to assist you. While you are saving Johansson, they can take out Spiffo."

"Dude, you shouldn't kill people. Like Svenson said, it's a rubber band of destruction."

"Enough. That is my offer. Take it or leave it."

"Fine. We'll take it," said JJ.

"Good. Now leave me."

"Hey, bro, can I add one more clause to the agreement," said Krusty. "No more strip searches."

“Out!” shouted Macbeth pointing a regal finger towards the door and the three of them returned to the bar for a well needed whisky.

Chapter 7

It was the fifth and final day of the mission and for the third day in a row it was JJ's phone which woke him. This time the alarm was set to silent and he was brought to consciousness by a tingling vibration in his upper leg. He pulled the phone out of his pants pocket and switched off the alarm. To his left, Svenson snored gently while to his right Krusty snored loudly. They were back in one of the meat lockers in Macbeth HQ where they had been invited to spend the night by Snake. The plan of attack had been set the preceding evening. They would launch the rescue mission for Johansson and Amber mid-morning and then head to the final ceremony of the Global Congress in the afternoon. JJ had retired early giving the truthful excuse that he hadn't had a full night's sleep in two days. But he also had an ulterior motive; a plan that he was about to put into action and that plan involved waking up at five AM. He was about to go intelligence gathering.

The first hurdle was going to be whether or not the door to the room they were sleeping in had been locked. It was pitch black and JJ turned on the light from his phone holding his hand over the bulb enough to block most of the light and stop Krusty and Svenson from waking up while still providing enough illumination to guide him over to the door. He pushed down as softly as he could on the large metal handle and pulled. The door swung open noiselessly and he let himself out and closed it behind him. The corridor was also unlit but there was some light emanating from the bar area about twenty metres away. This was going to be the next hurdle. Was there anybody awake at this time? If so, he would have to abort.

He turned off the light on his phone and crept up along the wall as quietly as possible until he approached the entrance to the bar where he slowly stuck his head around the corner to see if anybody was around. The light was coming from the two large fridges behind the bar which held the beer and other beverages. The room itself was empty and so he made his way past the pool tables and the stage which brought back memories of pink bathrobes and large men urinating. On the other side of the main room was the hallway, the final hurdle, that led to Macbeth's room. He had no particular idea what he would find in there. But he figured that within the cupboard or the chest of drawers of the dressing table there could be some insight, some snippet of information, some clue that could be useful.

Unlike the previous day, the door to the room was now closed. JJ stood beside it and weighed the odds. What chance the door was alarmed? Or booby-trapped? What chance Macbeth was actually inside sleeping? What chance there were armed goons? He held his ear to the door hoping for some information but quickly realised that no sound was going to make it through the three inches of hard metal. He would have to take a leap of faith. He squeezed down on the handle and gently pushed the door inwards.

There was no alarm, no booby trap and nobody in the room. JJ closed the door behind him and tiptoed past the throne and towards the furniture on the far wall. He opened a few drawers here and there to find articles of clothing, all black in colour as far as he could tell in the dim light of his phone. The toy box actually contained the kinds of things you would expect a young girl to have including dolls and even a couple of toy guns and cars. After some minutes, he was running out of things to look at and came to a last chest of drawers besides a cupboard. He opened the top one and shone the torch of his phone down into it. His bottom jaw dropped. He reached down and picked up the photo that was sitting on top of a pile of papers and held it up to the full light of the phone turning the phone a few times as if that would confirm that what his eyes were seeing was real and not an accident of the light. He stared at it with amazement for some time thinking through what it meant and when he'd finally come to terms with it he ruffled through the other items in the drawers. There was nothing else of interest and so he put the photo in his pocket, closed the drawer and crept out of the room.

Back with his two snoring mates, JJ walked over to his mattress and lay down with the intention of perhaps getting another hour of sleep before things kicked off for the day. But his mind was racing. The photo changed everything. He spent the next hour working through the ramifications of this new bit of information and developing a fresh plan of attack for the day ahead.

About an hour later, JJ got up and switched on the light in the room. The harsh bright fluorescent globes did nothing to rouse his two snoring companions and so he set about achieving that aim with the help of his foot.

"Oi. Wake up."

"Dude, what the fuck. It's not time yet," said Krusty who had no idea what time it was.

"It's almost time and we need to have a talk."

Krusty and Svenson, who had chosen to spend the evening in the bar rather than join JJ in going to bed early, slowly made their way into an upright position. JJ dragged over a couple of chairs for them to sit on in the hope that this would wake them up.

"We need to stop Macbeth's goons from killing Spiffo," said JJ once he was satisfied they were back in the land of the living. "And we can't kill Todhammerstein either."

"It was your idea to kill Todhammerstein," said Svenson.

"Yeah, but I was just saying that to Macbeth so she would help us to rescue Amber and Johansson."

"Hang on a second, bro," said Krusty. "We can stop the killing of Todhammerstein because we're the ones that are supposed to do it. How can we stop Macbeth's goons from taking out Spiffo?"

"We have to talk them out of it."

"Talk them out of it? Err, dude, I'm not sure if you've been paying attention, but these guys are kinda fanatical. Look at McCutcheon, for example. Think you could have talked him out it?"

"Maybe. We never tried cos we never knew what he was gonna do."

"Why do you care about Spiffo all of a sudden? The guy's a dick."

"I told you, new information has come to light."

"What?"

"I can't tell you yet."

"Would this new information help to change the minds of Macbeth's goons?"

"Probably," said JJ who hadn't thought about this angle. "But we can't tell them either yet or it might spoil the main mission."

"What's the main mission again?"

"To save Amber and Johansson."

"Oh, yeah. I forgot about them."

"Well this is a giant fuckup," said Svenson not with any particular anger in his voice just as if he was stating a fact.

He got up off his chair and walked a few metres away where he began doing some star jumps.

"What are you doing?" asked JJ.

"My morning stretches," replied Svenson who began bending over to touch his toes.

"So, recapping the plan," said Krusty ignoring his Norwegian counterpart, "we save Johansson and Amber while talking Macbeth's goons out of killing Spiffo and then go to the ceremony and just do nothing."

"There won't be any need to go to the ceremony," said JJ. "It would be better to go into hiding so that Macbeth can't find us."

"Into hiding?"

"Johansson will be able to give us protection."

"You think? We're about to screw over the country's number of one mafia organisation, dude. Personally, I'd rather have them protecting me from the government than the other way round."

"Well, I'm not killing Todhammerstein."

"Let me do it," said Svenson in between sit-ups.

"Nobody's killing anybody," said JJ. "We'll figure out what the best plan of action is once we've saved Johansson and Amber."

Krusty checked the clock on his phone.

"We've got about five minutes til shooting practice."

The shooting practice had been discussed the day before after it was revealed that none of them had ever fired a gun before. Snake had instructed the three associates who would accompany them to rub out Spiffo to give them shooting lessons first thing in the morning. JJ stood up and caste a sideways glance over at Svenson who was now doing a set of push-ups.

"How are we gonna convince these guys not to shoot Spiffo?" said JJ repeating the problem as if hoping a solution would come.

"Y'know, I remember when we were smoking weed with McCutcheon, I made some crack about how he was taking orders from a little girl and he got really pissed and wanted to fight me and stuff," said Krusty.

"That's it!" said JJ snapping his fingers.

"What? We're gonna tease them into not doing it?"

"No. Yes. Well, maybe. But first we'll get them stoned. Have you got some weed on you?"

"Yeah. But, dude, it's not even eight o'clock in the morning."

"That's never stopped you before."

"I guess not."

"No, this is perfect. We'll get them stoned and then start asking them questions and putting doubts into their mind. Maybe even play on their paranoia or whatever. Whaddya think?"

"Sounds like a long shot, bro. But it's my kind of long shot."

Krusty pulled out a bag of weed and a cigarette paper and began rolling a joint. A few minutes later the door swung open and three large men in black leather outfits and tattoos entered the room.

"Alright, ladies, it's time for you to learn how to be men," said the first guy who compensated for a lack of hair on his head by an extra-large red beard that hung down to his chest. He was wearing the obligatory Macbeth outfit of black leather everything.

"What's this shit?" said the second guy pointing at Svenson who was now sitting on the floor touching his toes.

"Sensei over here's doing some yoga," said the third.

"Is yoga Japanese?" asked the second.

"Shut the fuck up, both of you," said the first. "C'mon, Cinderella. It's time for the ball."

"Are you ready to learn to be a killer?" asked the second as he slapped JJ on the shoulder.

"Yep," said JJ trying to sound confident and failing.

"What about you, matey?" said the bearded one to Krusty.

"Absolutely, bro. Ready to shoot the shit outta some shit."

Krusty lit up his joint and took a long drag.

"You blokes want a toke?" he asked holding up the joint.

"It's a bit early in the morning. But, hey, it's six o'clock somewhere and all that."

The each took a deep toke before passing it on.

"Good stuff. That tastes like Krusty's Special," said the first guy.

"That's cos it is," said Krusty. "And *I* am Krusty."

"No way. You're the Krusty in Krusty's Special?"

"That's right, bro."

"Did you hear that, Tommy? This guy's Krusty. The guy who grows Krusty's Special."

"Wow, we got a real life legend in the group. Alright, Krusty, let's show you how to shoot."

***

"Mate, you shoot like a one-legged wombat on LSD," shouted the bearded man, who had earlier introduced himself as Macca.

This was apparently the funniest thing the other two, Tommy and Pincer, had heard in their lives as they doubled over with laughter as JJ removed his earmuffs and put the gun down on the table next to him. Krusty's Special was doing its work and the men were onto about their fourth joint which had done nothing to improve the quality of their teaching method which consisted in sitting back and making fun of how bad JJ and the others were at shooting. Despite the poor quality of instruction, JJ had still gotten to the point where he could now reliably hit the target which was some improvement on his part.

He joined the others at the table and gave a searching look to Krusty who gave a slight nod in return to indicate it was time to begin the psychological gamesmanship.

"So, look, dudes, there's one thing we've been wondering about and it's a little bit of an awkward question."

"More awkward than this son of a bitch's shooting technique," said the third goon to more bouts of laughter.

"Nah, not that awkward," said Krusty winking at JJ. "Nah, we were just wondering how you guys feel about taking orders from a twelve year old girl. Y'know, isn't that a bit weird and stuff?"

Before he knew it, Krusty was on his feet thrust upwards by two clenched fists grasped around the collar of his shirt.

"What are you trying to say, funny guy?" asked Macca.

"Nothing, bro. Nothing at all."

Macca slowly released his grip and glared at Krusty as they both slowly resumed their seats. There was a few moments of awkward silence before Tommy, who seemed to have been thinking about the question, spoke in an earnest tone.

"Y'know, I've thought about that sometimes. Like, here we are, a room full of grown men, trained warriors and fighters, and we just do whatever she says. It's not even an age thing, just a basic respect thing, y'know?"

"Yeah, and she never says a kind word that one. I've never had a compliment or a thank you or a single word of encouragement. It's just do this, do that, kill this guy, throw that guy off a bridge," added Pincer.

"I've never thought about it like that," said Macca who dropped into a thoughtful silence staring at the table in front of him.

Krusty gave JJ an over-to-you look.

"Right, so, ummm, y'know, we were thinking, about that ordering you to kill people thing, y'know, it's really not right to kill this Spiffo guy. I mean, think about it, he's never done anything to us and he's never done anything to you, right?"

"I've never even heard of him before," agreed Tommy.

"Exactly. And until a couple of days ago, I'd never heard of him either. So, we don't need to kill him, do we? Just because Macbeth says so, doesn't make it right."

"No, I guess it doesn't."

"I mean," added JJ getting encouragement from the response of the men, "this guy probably has a wife and kids. He's just trying to put food on the table."

"He's right. It wouldn't be polite to kill him."

"No, it would be distinctly impolite."

"Having said that," added Krusty, "I think we should still beat him up. A few nice punches to the guts, maybe even a slap across the face or a corky or something."

"Absolutely," agreed JJ. "A bit of rough stuff is fine. What do you say, guys? It'll be more fun that way. I mean, killing somebody with a gun, it's almost too easy."

"You should torture him a little too," said Svenson.

"Great idea. In fact, take him into a room and give him a good going over. Take your time with it and have some fun. Whaddya say?"

JJ looked at the three expectantly.

"I could go with that."

"Sounds like plan."

"Count me in."

"Perfect," said JJ getting up and clapping his hands together like a salesman that had just sold a lemon to a sucker. "So, we'll just beat him up. We won't kill him, ok? Now that that's sorted out, I think it's time to go?"

"I reckon so. Let's go and get the gear, boys," said Macca and the three men got up and walked out the room.

"Dude, I can't believe that worked so easily."

"I know," said JJ. "But listen, how much weed have you got left?"

Krusty pulled out his plastic bag and held it up. There was a smattering of green in the bottom.

"Not much, bro."

"Svenson, you got any?"

Svenson shook his head.

"Damn. Alright, look, we need to keep these guys stoned so they don't revert back to their old selves. So, I dunno, just space it out as best you can but keep the joints rolling til it's over."

"Don't worry, dude. Just leave it to Dr Krusty, PhD in THC."

***

The black van with the dark tinted windows chugged into life as Macca got into the back and closed the rear door behind him.

"Let's go," he shouted to the front where Snake was seated in the passenger seat.

The driver shifted into gear and slowly drove up the ramp towards the light of day. In the back sat JJ, Krusty and Svenson with the Macca, Tommy and Pincer. For the first time, JJ was not made to wear a blindfold. A strange omission, he thought, given the rigor with which it was enforced on previous occasions. It made him a little nervous. They were about to learn the location of HQ even though the deal was that this would be their final mission with the Macbeth Corporation. He might have forgiven Macca and the other two who were still probably a bit stoned. But Snake himself was on the mission too and he was not the type who would overlook such a thing. Was Snake planning to rub them out afterwards or did he just forget? In any case, JJ's curiosity was running on high and he tried as discreetly as possible to get a view through the front windscreen, there being no windows in the back of the van. He knew already that they must be in Kirribilli or a neighbouring suburb and this was confirmed by the residential appearance of townhouses, apartments and expensive cars parked on the narrow street. He looked for some kind of landmark that he would recognise but this was a longshot unless they happened to be on the same street where Amber lived.

They had only been underway a minute or two when the sweet smell of dope smoke made its way throughout the van. Krusty passed the joint on to Macca and from there it was passed around the back. Snake turned around from the front with a look of disapproval to see Tommy taking a toke.

"Isn't it a bit early for that?" he asked with furrowed brow.

"It's 6 o'clock somewhere, bro," replied Krusty.

"I didn't realise you guys were such potheads?" said Snake to the three associates.

Macca shrugged.

"Krusty here's the king of weed. He's been keeping us well supplied all morning."

"Has he just?" said Snake looking curiously at JJ who didn't return his gaze.

"Why are we back here?" JJ asked, keen to change the subject but also noticing that they were coming to a stop right in front of the park opposite 12 Alice Street.

"You wanted to rescue Johansson and your girlfriend, this is where they are being held."

"Of course," said JJ as if it was obvious in hindsight. "Right where Spiffo can keep an eye on them."

"Exactly. And speaking of Spiffo. Here comes our man right now exactly as our intelligence indicated."

JJ squinted through the windscreen to see the familiar figure of Spiffo walking in through the large double doors of 12 Alice Street accompanied by a couple of other men in suits who looked more like agents than fellow politicians.

"Are those agents going to be with him the whole time?" asked JJ.

"I assume so," answered Snake. "But that's why you've got the boys here."

The "boys" broke out into a bout of giggling as Tommy finished off the last of the joint.

"Oi!," shouted Snake like an angry schoolteacher. "Pull yourselves together. This isn't the goddamn girl guides. It's game time."

The men in the back stopped their giggling and attempted to look serious.

"Our intelligence indicates that Spiffo is now occupying the Prime Minister's office. Do you know where that is?"

"Sure do. It's on the top floor," said JJ.

"Good. That's where you'll find Spiffo and also where you'll find Johansson. If our sources are correct, he's being held in one of the other offices on the top floor."

"How can we get to the top floor without being seen, bro?" asked Krusty.

"There's an emergency stairwell," said Svenson.

"Dude, that's twenty stories up."

"We can't take the elevator. It's too risky," said JJ.

"How are we gonna get to the stairwell?"

"We can go back through the hole in the wall," said Svenson.

"Hole in the wall?" asked Snake.

"It's how we got out of the building in the first place," explained JJ. "We knocked a sewage pipe out of the wall in our room."

"The staircase is right near the door to our room too," added Svenson.

"Alright. Sounds like you've got a plan, gentlemen. I suggest you put it into action. Our intelligence indicates Spiffo will be here for the morning and will head to the congress ceremony about lunch time. That gives you a good three hours to do the job."

"Let's do this," shouted Macca who threw open the rear door on the van and they all jumped out.

"This way," said JJ as he led them around the outskirts of the park until they were standing opposite the rear corner of 12 Alice Street where their old room was.

JJ had a quick look around for any cops or agents and, seeing none, crossed the road. The building was set back about ten metres from the footpath and there was decent visual cover in the form of a collection of large shrubs and trees. They walked over and took up a position on the wall about five metres from the hole.

"Wait here while I take a quick look inside," he told the others.

He walked over beside the hole, crouched down and peered through the wall. The room was not empty. He could see some human figures inside but it wasn't until his eyes adjusted to the light and he stuck his head in a little further that he could see that it was none other than Bennings, Bennetson and Anderson. They were inspecting the hydroponics setup in the room. Bennings himself had a number of plastic bags which contained samples of the kale while there were also a number of glass jars containing the familiar brown and yellow fluid. Anderson looked to be inspecting the equipment from underneath as if looking for some kind of modification that might have been made. In any case, it didn't look like they were going to be leaving soon.

JJ pulled his head out of the wall and returned to the others.

"Bad news. Bennings and the other two are in there snooping around."

"That cocksucker?" said Krusty.

"He's stealing my ideas," added Svenson.

"Let's kick his arse."

"I don't think that's a good idea. Bennings is not what we're here for. Besides, it takes too long to get through the hole. By the time we got even one person into the room they could run off and sound the alarm."

"So, how else are we gonna get in?"

JJ pulled his wallet out of his pocket and took a small white card from it.

"I reckon this will still work."

"Our building passes? Wouldn't they have cancelled those?"

"I doubt they're that organised. Anyway, it'll only take a minute to find out. C'mon."

JJ led them around the corner and over to the rear entrance door to the basement where he skipped down the few stairs to the bottom and held the card over the scanner which promptly flashed green. JJ held his finger up to signify that he would take a look first. He cracked open the door. There was nobody in the hall. He turned to the others.

"Let me go ahead a little bit to make sure the coast is clear. I'll wave you through."

Krusty came down the steps and held the door open while JJ started his journey across the hall. Their destination was the white door marked "Fire Escape" on the far wall. It was right out the front of the door to Team Melbourne's room. As JJ got closer he realised that the door was open which meant they were going to have to take a chance that Bennings and the others would see them. All the other doors to the other rooms that had been used for the competition were closed. JJ took a quick look up the staircase to see if there were any guards but there seemed to be nobody around. The whole area was deathly silent and he had to try his best to keep his footsteps inaudible. He turned and waved for the others to enter and then continued onwards towards the door to their old room.

He took up a place beside the doorframe and turned back to the others who were now near the steps holding up his hand to signal for them to wait there and then turned back and slowly stuck his head around the door to get a view into the room. Bennetson and Anderson were still pottering around at the rear of the room while Bennings was nowhere to be seen. JJ figured he must but underneath the hydroponics system investigating. If so, there was no time to spare. He skipped over to the fire escape door and pushed it open carefully hoping like hell it wasn't hooked up to any kind of alarm. He stepped inside the stairwell to make sure nobody was on the steps inside and then turned to wave the others in only to find Bennings standing about three metres in front of him with his hands on his hips and a stupid smile on his face.

"A good criminal should know not to return to the scene of the crime, Mr Wochensky. But that's not your real name, is it?"

"I dunno what you're taking about," said JJ who tried to keep a straight face as he watched Krusty, Svenson and, more importantly, the three large tattooed Macbeth associates quietly creep up behind Bennings, who apparently hadn't seen them.

"I got several emails from our horticultural associates in Melbourne yesterday. They saw the photos of the competition winners and, whaddya know, the names didn't match the faces. Anyway, they sent me a photo of the real Wochensky. Did you know he's a sixty three year old balding man with glasses?"

"No. I never met him."

"Who are you then?"

"It doesn't matter who I am".

"I guess not. Once I call the guards you'll disappear and nobody will ever see you again."

"I wouldn't be so sure," said JJ as Macca grabbed Bennings and lifted him off the ground like a giant squid taking its prey.

Bennings tried to scream but with Macca's hand clasped firmly over his mouth his voice went nowhere. JJ waved them into the Team Melbourne room.

"Get those two," he shouted pointing to the end of the room where Anderson and Bennetson apparently had no idea what had been going on outside the door.

Bennetson threw her arms up and started squealing while Anderson showed surprising athleticism by grabbing onto the pipe above the hole in the wall and swinging his legs through. Unfortunately for him, his stomach was even wider than Krusty's and he managed nothing more than to get himself stuck. Tommy helped him out of the hole and they lined the three of them against the wall.

“What are we gonna do with them?” asked Krusty.

“We can’t leave them in here. They’ll get out through the wall,” said Svenson.

“Two of them might. But not this fat arse,” said Tommy giving Anderson a thump on the stomach.

“Let’s just shoot ‘em,” said Macca pulling a pistol out and holding it to Bennings’ head who looked like he was about to faint at the sight of the gun.

“Woah, no!” said JJ holding up his hands. “We agreed no killing, didn’t we?”

“I s’pose,” said Macca who sounded genuinely disappointed as he put the gun away.

“I know, we’ll lock them in their own room,” said JJ.

Bennings, Bennetson and Anderson were swept out into the hall and into the Team Sydney room room as if by a strong wind.

“Take their phones,” said JJ. “We need to make sure they can’t alert anybody.”

“Even better,” said Krusty with a big smile. “Strip ‘em”.

Macca, Tommy and Pincer, who had conducted numerous initiation ceremonies back at Macbeth HQ and thus were experts in stripping people of their clothes, were happy to comply with this command and before long Bennings and co were down to their underwear which brought a smile even to JJ’s face. They collected the phones and handed them to JJ.

“When was the last time you saw Spiffo?” JJ asked Bennings.

“I’m not telling you anything.”

JJ raised his eyebrow and then gave a wave to Macca who promptly twisted Bennings’ arm literally and metaphorically.

“About half an hour ago,” wheezed Bennings as he tried to squeeze out of Macca’s grip.

“Where was he?”

"In his office."

"You mean Johansson's office."

"It's Spiffo's office now."

"We'll see about that. And where's Johansson and his daughter?"

"Locked in an office just near Spiffo's."

"Are there any police up there?"

"Not that I saw."

"Fine," said JJ who bent down and picked up Bennings' pants where he removed the keys from the pocket and found the key to the door of the room which he removed from the keychain.

"Thanks for your help," said JJ with a smile as he turned to leave the room.

"There's just one thing I wanna know," said Bennings as JJ got to the door while the others filed out into the hall. "Did you really use shit to fertilise the kale?"

"You saw that for yourself," replied JJ.

"I can't believe it," said Bennings shaking his head.

"Well, now you know what the Winfield Method is. Try it yourself sometime."

JJ closed the door and turned the key which he left in the lock and then ran over to the emergency stairwell where Svenson was holding open the door.

***

Svenson was the first to reach the twentieth floor. Clearly his morning stretching routine was paying dividends for his fitness. He was followed by Macca, Tommy and Pincer. JJ was lagging behind although not because of a lack of fitness on his part. The lack of fitness was being demonstrated by Krusty who had begun panting at about the fifth floor which had turned into a gasping at about the twelfth and had now descended into a wheezing. JJ hung back to have a quick word with him.

"Hey, I need you to roll another joint and get those three smoking again. I think they're straightening up with all this exercise and I need them nice and relaxed when we go in."

Krusty was wheezing like an off kilter pedestal fan.

"Wha....? Dude, I......gimme a min..."

Krusty collapsed on the step half a flight away from the top and leant back against the wall with his head back trying to suck in the air.

"This whole building smells like shit," said Macca from the top step.

"It's not surprising," said Svenson. "Now that the sewage is no longer flowing through our hydroponics setup, it will be getting backed up in the pipes."

"It's making me nauseous."

JJ walked up the remaining stairs to where the others were standing.

"Now, remember, no guns and no killing," he said sounding like an over protective father figure.

"Sure. No guns," replied Macca in a tone that made it clear there would be guns.

JJ thought about pressing the point but remembered the agents who had entered the building and figured that having some firepower at their disposal wasn't the worst strategy in the circumstances. He looked back at Krusty who had more or less regained his breath but realised smoking a joint now would be weird and probably counterproductive. He figured it was better to cut his losses and not wait for another joint to be rolled.

"Alright. Johansson's office is in the corner. We turn right as we go through the door and it's at the end of the corridor. Just walk naturally so we don't draw attention to ourselves if anybody is around."

JJ realised how ridiculous this sounded as he looked at the three tall men clad in black leather and tattoos who were about as inconspicuous in an office building as a pride of lions walking through a herd of zebras.

"Krusty, you right to go?"

Krusty gave a viable-looking thumbs up and pulled himself up off the concrete floor. JJ waited for him to get to the top of the steps before swinging open the door and ushering them inside. They walked straight into three other mean-looking leather-clad dudes who were standing just a few metres from the door with guns drawn. In the middle was Cody and beside him were the two others that JJ recognised from the club in the city.

"You?" said JJ with a mixture of shock and disapproval.

"Surprise," said Cody with fake enthusiasm. "Now, every-body get their hands up where I can see them."

JJ and the others raised their hands in the air.

"What are you doing here?" asked JJ.

"Arresting you."

"Why would you arrest us?"

Cody removed something from his pocket and held it up for them to see. It was a police badge.

"You're cops?"

"Special operations. We do undercover work keeping an eye on extremist groups and enemies of the state looking for people just like you lot."

"You work for Spiffo?"

"Now you're getting the picture. Max, if you'd like to do the honours of removing these gentlemen from their weapons."

The guy on the right moved over and began patting down Macca and the others removing the guns, knives and other weapons as he found them.

"How did you know we were coming?" asked JJ.

"Remember those cameras we put up in the basement? They came in handy after all."

JJ nodded as he remembered the location of the cameras on the wall which must have picked up the whole show with Bennings earlier on.

"You're a good actor," he said to Cody. "I would never have picked you as a cop."

"Thank you for the compliment. Now if you'll be so kind as to follow me. I'll re-introduce you to some friends of yours while we figure out what to do with you."

Cody led them down the corridor where there was a large meeting room. He unlocked the door and pushed it open. Inside, Johansson and Amber were sitting on a couple of chairs at a large boardroom table.

"JJ!" said Amber jumping up and running over to hug him as he entered.

"Well, isn't this just touching," said Cody watching on. "Melts your heart, doesn't it, Max?"

Max grinned as he shoved Macca into the room. With everybody in, Cody and the other two walked out. The door closed behind them, there was a click of the lock and the flicker of shadows on the opaque glass panes of the meeting room as they walked back down the corridor.

"Where've you been?" asked Amber pulling herself away from JJ.

"It's a long story. I'll tell you later," said JJ.

He looked around the room. On the one side there was the Prime Minister of the country, on the other a group of mafia thugs and in the middle some weirdos from the bush.

"Maybe we should introduce ourselves to each other," said JJ.

"With your real names this time?" asked Johansson from his chair near the boardroom table.

"Yes, real names," said JJ.

"Well, let me start," said Johansson getting out of his chair. "I'm Florian".

"I'm JJ."

"Hey, bro. I'm Krusty."

"Svenson, at your service," said Svenson giving a small bow.

Johansson shook hands with each one in turn and then moved over to the Macbeth associates and held out his hand to shake. They looked back with confused expressions.

"I dunno, mate. Technically, we're supposed to hate you," said Macca.

"Yeah, we were talking about assassinating you at one point," added Tommy.

"Are you still going to assassinate me?" asked Johansson.

"Umm, I don't think so."

"Good. Please don't."

Johansson gave a smile as he shook the men's hands and exchanged names.

"Well, know we know each other. Tell us, how did you end up getting captured?" he asked returning to his seat at the table.

"We came back here to rescue you both," said JJ. "We were almost there until those undercover cops busted us."

"I know. I can't believe it," said Amber. "Cody was in here earlier today questioning us. I was sure he was some anarchist or something and all the time I've known him he was a cop."

"Pretty sure his name's not Cody," said JJ.

"He's good at his job," said Johansson. "I guess the next question is what are we going to do now? We seem to be in a pretty pickle."

"So, you support us, Mr Johansson?" asked JJ.

"Please, call me Florian. And, yes, I support you. Amber and I have had a lot of time to talk over the last day. She's told me everything about what you've been up to. Very impressive."

"But, I saw you with Todhammerstein at the competition. You were talking about how great kale is and the all the stuff about yields and all that. I thought you were a supporter of the Global Council?"

"You do realise that the job of a politician involves pretending to like people you despise while talking a bunch of crap you don't believe in," said Johansson with a smile.

"Uhh, ok."

"Look, I've done my best to try and ward off the encroachment of the Global Council on our country but there's only so much that can be done especially with zealots like Spiffo around."

"He's trying to steal the Prime Ministership?" asked Svenson.

"That's exactly what he's trying to do. I'm guessing his plan is simply to show up at the Congress today, announce that he is now the Prime Minister and then use that illusion to get rid of me probably by tying something around my feet and throwing me in the Harbour. That seems to be the fashionable way to do it these days."

"So, we need to get to Spiffo before he gets to the Congress," said Krusty.

"That's gonna be a little hard given that we are locked in a room."

Macca turned around a took a couple of steps over to the window which he prodded a couple of times with his hand.

"I reckon we can smash through this," he said.

"Even if we do, they've got guns and we don't," said Amber.

"I think I know a way to get to Spiffo and it won't require any violence at all," said JJ.

"What's that?" asked Johansson.

"It'll work better if I don't tell you. We just need to get Spiffo in here. Is there any way we can lure him in?"

"I can lure him," said Johannsson who walked over to the door and started thumping on it.

"Guards! Guards! Tell Spiffo I've changed my mind. If he brings in the documents now, I'll sign them."

A couple of shadows on the other side of the glass seemed to indicate that the message was heard and was being relayed back to Spiffo.

"Documents?" asked JJ.

"To resign from the Prime Ministership and give it over to him."

"I thought you wouldn't want to do that, bro?" asked Krusty.

"I don't. So, whatever JJ has in mind had better work."

Johansson gave JJ a smile and a slap on the shoulder and sat back down at the boardroom table.

A few minutes later several shadows appeared in the glass window and there was a click in the lock after which the door opened. Cody and his two lackeys walked in and took up positions next to the door with guns drawn. JJ and Amber moved over to stand beside Johansson who was seated while Krusty, Svenson and the others moved away from the door on the other side of the table. Spiffo walked in with some papers and a pen in hand. He took a look around the room recognising JJ, Krusty and Svenson but turning up his eyebrows, and his nose, at Macca and the other two.

"Who are these goons?" he asked.

"They belong to the Macbeth Corporation," answered Cody.

"Ah, yes. I've heard the name. Some kind of mob outfit, right?"

"Correct. The Macbeth Corporation is the number one mafia organisation in the country. One of the few we have been unable to infiltrate."

"That's cos we're the best," said Macca proudly.

"If you were so good, you wouldn't be standing here," snapped Cody back.

"Put that gun down and we'll find out who's good or not," snarled Macca.

"Ok, ok. That's enough of that," said Spiffo sitting down at the table and laying out the papers and pen. "We've got some business to attend to, don't we, Mr Johansson?"

"I have some information about the Macbeth Corporation that you might be interested in, Mr Spiffo," said JJ. "It'll help you a lot with your infiltration efforts."

"What!?" said Macca in a threatening tone of voice.

"You best keep your mouth shut," warned Tommy. "Ratting out to the authorities is punishable by death according to the Corporation code of conduct."

"Well, well. This sounds nice and juicy," said Cody. "Let's hear it."

"I'll bet you've never seen a photograph of Macbeth, have you?" JJ asked Cody.

"No. That's another thing that has tripped us up. Apparently Macbeth is a bit nuts about the subject and has had a number of people taken out just for having a camera in his vicinity."

"That's right. Well, I happen to have a photograph of Macbeth with me right now."

JJ took several steps towards Macca and the others. He pulled the photograph out and covered one side of it with his hand before holding it up to them.

"Boys, can you confirm that the person in this photo is Macbeth."

JJ gave them a wink and a nod to encourage them to answer.

"Yeah, that's right," said Macca through gritted teeth.

JJ walked back over to his starting point besides Johansson so that he was a couple of metres in front of Spiffo who was on the other side of the boardroom table.

"Would you like to see the photo of Macbeth?" he asked.

Spiffo, who was no stranger to intrigue and politicking, had the look of a man who knew he was being set up but also couldn't figure out how. In the end, curiosity got the better of him.

"Alright, let's see it."

JJ held up the photo and Spiffo's poker face seemed to split into equal parts horror and anger.

"What's this bullshit?" he shouted standing up angrily.

JJ removed his hand from the other half of the photo and showed it to the room. There were audible gasps from all directions including even Cody. The photo was a family portrait that had been professionally shot with proper background. There were just two members of the family, both dressed formally and smiling for the camera: on the left was Sam Spiffo and on the right was his twelve year old daughter, known to everybody else in the room as Pickles Macbeth, although her real name was Samantha.

"Isn't that your daughter?" asked Johansson.

"Yes, it's my goddamn daughter," answered Spiffo.

"Wait, you're telling me that Macbeth, the leader of the Corporation, is this son of a bitch's daughter?" asked Macca gesturing towards Spiffo.

"That's right," said JJ. "And I'm ninety-nine percent sure that the Corporation headquarters are located beneath Mr Spiffo's house just five minutes away from here."

"But, hang on," said Tommy. "Macbeth sent us here to kill Spiffo."

"She wanted to kill me?" asked Spiffo.

"Bullet through the head, mate," said Macca using his middle and forefinger to mime a gun.

"Oh, man. That's fucked up. Even by mob standards."

"I thought mobsters were s'posed to protect their family?"

Spiffo, who had initially reacted with anger had quickly descended through the stages of grief and ended up in depression. He slumped over in his chair staring at the table in front of him.

"It all makes sense," he mumbled to himself. "Oh, what have I done?"

A gentle sobbing started that was so pathetic that everybody in the room turned away slightly. Cody and the other two undercover cops even lowered their guns as if in sympathy with their boss.

"Look, mate, it's hard work to raise a daughter as a single father," said Johansson from the other side of the table. "Especially when you're working seven days a week. Believe me, I know. Amber and I have had our troubles. That's how she got mixed up with your undercover agents here in some filthy underground club in the city."

"We were just doing our jobs," said Cody with a slight look of embarrassment on his face.

Johansson swung his chair around the table and put his arm around Spiffo's shoulder who was still sobbing.

Everybody in the room had lowered their gaze at the scene playing out in front of them. As a result, nobody noticed the shadow that was moving across the opaque glass of the meeting room until it materialised into human form in the doorway.

"Well, doesn't this just warm the cockles of your heart."

JJ looked up to see Snake standing in the doorway looking over Johansson and Spiffo. He was holding a handgun which he pointed towards Cody and the other two cops.

"I need you to drop those weapons real quick, gentlemen," he said.

The cops, who had already lowered their guns, reluctantly dropped them on the floor.

"Now move over there beside my associates."

Snake waved his gun in the direction of Macca. Cody and the other two walked the few metres to the other side of the room while Snake took a step inside with the doorway behind him.

"How did you get in, Snake?" asked JJ.

"I slid in through your hole in the wall, Mr JJ. Much obliged for that. I knew I couldn't trust these clowns over here," he said gesturing towards Macca. "And I knew I definitely couldn't trust you. I dunno what game you thought you were playing, Mr JJ, but you've done me a big favour by gathering all the people I need to kill into one place. Very convenient."

"What? You're gonna kill us too?" asked Macca.

"You know the rules, Mac. No loose ends."

"But, new information has come to light, Snake," objected Tommy. "New information about the Corporation. It's all a lie. Tell him, JJ."

JJ held up the photo of Spiffo and his daughter so Snake could see.

"Macbeth is not who you think she is, Snake. She's the daughter of Sam Spiffo. This man right here. A federal politician."

"I knew that already," said Snake.

"Huh? You knew that?"

"Of course. Who do you think has been coaching her this whole time? Who do you think has really been running the Macbeth Corporation? Did you think a self-obsessed twelve year old with daddy issues has been running the nation's biggest mafia organisation?"

"I guess not," said JJ who realised that it did sound ridiculous although no more ridiculous than anything else that had happened in the past two weeks. "So, it was your idea to kill Johansson and Spiffo?"

"As always, you catch on fast, Mr JJ. Unfortunately for you, though, you've been a step behind the whole way. It's a shame. Someone with your brains could have been a real asset to the Corporation."

"I never wanted to join in the first place," said JJ.

"Well, you did. And now you'll have to pay the consequences. No loose ends, I'm afraid."

Snake aimed the gun at JJ.

"Hang on! You need me. You need me to kill Todhammerstein at the Congress. I've still got the passes."

"No, that's the beauty of it, Mr JJ. Little Samantha is going to do that for me. See, as the daughter of Mr Spiffo here, she has her own ticket to the Congress and she'll be sitting right next to Todhammerstein."

"She's gonna shoot him?"

"No, she's going to infect him with a killer virus."

"In a white spray bottle?"

"No," laughed Snake. "See, the idea was right all along. We do want to kill Todhammerstein with a virus but this time we'll do it properly using a device so small and innocent-looking carried by a girl so small and innocent-looking that nobody will ever suspect a thing. But Todhammerstein is going to cark it right in the middle of his closing address to the world and with any luck we'll take out a few of the other Global Council members with him."

"And then you'll take over the country?"

"No, Samantha Spiffo will take over the country. It'll be a great story. A daughter in mourning at the tragic death of her father steps up to take the reins of power. All hail Queen Spiffo."

"You're sick," snarled Spiffo.

"You should thank me," smiled Snake. "I'm having your daughter do exactly what you've been trying to do. A Spiffo will be the leader of the country after all."

"So, what's in this then?" asked JJ holding up the white spray bottle which he still had in his other pocket.

"Just water, my friend."

JJ was standing on the side of the boardroom table, less than three metres away from Snake. He raised the white bottle and pressed down as hard as he could. As had happened with Todhammerstein, the spray travelled an impressive distance turning slightly upwards and going straight into Snake's nostrils.

"That's cute, Mr JJ," said Snake but no sooner had the words escaped his lips than he took a step back as if off balance slightly and held his hand up to his nose but it was too late. He bent over and let out a giant sneeze.

JJ seized the chance and rushed forward grabbing the wrist of the hand that was holding the gun with both his hands and pushing down with all his weight. Snake, who had several inches and about ten kilograms advantage over JJ, was caught off guard by the initial surprise but quickly regained his footing. He'd pulled the gun back into some kind of shooting position just in time to be gang tackled by Cody, Macca, Tommy, Pincer and the other two cops. By the time the melee broke up, Snake found himself pinned against the floor with Cody holding his gun. Cody pulled out a pair of handcuffs and he and the other two undercover cops dragged Snake from the room.

"Nice work, bro," said Krusty slapping JJ on the shoulder.

"How did you know that would work?" asked Amber.

"I didn't. But it worked on Todhammerstein a couple of days ago so I thought it was worth a try. He was gonna shoot me anyway."

"He was gonna shoot all of us," said Macca who sounded outraged at the idea. "What a betrayal."

"That's how things work in the mob, bro. Didn't you know?"

"I guess not."

"Well, that solves one of our problems," said Johansson. "But there's still one more to go."

"Macbeth?" said JJ then realised Spiffo was giving him a weird look. "I mean, Samantha Spiffo."

"That's right. If Snake can be relied on to have told the truth, and I think in this case he can, she's going to kill Todhammerstein."

"We have to stop her," said Spiffo jumping out of his seat.

"Why?" asked Krusty.

"What do you mean why? She's going to kill somebody. She's going to commit murder."

"Hasn't she been committing murders for years? I mean, as part of her job as leader of the mafia and stuff."

"I don't think so," said Macca. "Snake was responsible for all the day-to-day operations of the Corporation. Macbeth, I mean, Samantha, was more like the spiritual leader. She was only around for the ceremonies and to give speeches."

"Would you be prepared to testify to that extent?" asked Spiffo.

"Woah, hang on. What do you mean testify?"

"There has to be an investigation and a trial. I want the people who corrupted my daughter to be held accountable."

"Better look in the mirror, dude," said Krusty.

"Now, now, Sam," said Johansson, "I don't think it will be necessary to have any formal investigation. In fact, I'm sure it will be in everybody's interest to handle this as discreetly as possible."

"What about us?" asked Tommy.

"As far as I'm concerned, you've already atoned for any crimes you may have committed by your actions in this very room. Sam, do you agree?"

"I guess so," said Spiffo whose mind seemed elsewhere. "What time is it?" he said more to himself than anybody else then decided to answer the question by checking his own watch.

"I've got to go. I've got to find Samantha and stop her from going to the ceremony."

"Too late. She's already there," said Macca.

"But the ceremony doesn't start for a few hours yet."

"She's at the congress. We dropped her off earlier on. She's attending the workshops and meetings and all that crap. Snake has been planning this for weeks."

"Then I have to go to the Congress and get her out of there."

"Won't that create a scene?" asked Amber.

"I'll make up something about a family emergency."

"Hang on, can we stop for a minute and talk about the bigger picture here," said JJ. "Let's say Mr Spiffo here stops his daughter from killing Todhammerstein. The congress finishes without incident, the Global Council members fly back to wherever they came from and nobody is the wiser about all this. What happens to the Macbeth Corporation? I mean, we've arrested Snake and presumably Samantha won't be running it anymore."

"It'll be immediately shut down, of course," said Spiffo.

"You can't do that. We make our living from the Corporation," objected Macca.

"Me too," added Krusty.

"Me three," added Svenson.

"Me four," said JJ.

"Well, you'll have to find other ways to make a living," thundered Spiffo. "Bloody hell, we just exonerated you from all your crimes and now you're whinging about money."

"The problem is not just us, Mr Spiffo," continued JJ. "The Macbeth Corporation accounts for a large part of the Australian economy and not just for things that are illegal. I sell electrical goods. There's other people fixing cars, doing plumbing and other trades. Macbeth recently took over the banking services for Tittybong and other areas. If you shut down the Macbeth Corporation, it'll cause economic chaos especially in the country areas."

"We can look into nationalising it," suggested Johansson.

"Nationalising a criminal organisation?" asked Spiffo with raised eyebrows.

"It sounds like Macbeth is too big to fail."

"But isn't a large part of the reason why Macbeth exists in the first place because of the policies enforced by the government?" asked Amber. "If you get rid of those policies, legitimate businesses can return to fill those economic functions."

"Exactly," said JJ. "Let's take the cash thing. All you have to do is overturn the cash ban and re-open the city walls again and that problem goes away."

"I don't think we can do that," said Johansson.

"Why not?" asked Amber. "Aren't you two on the same team now. You're the two most powerful politicians in the country."

"I think you're overestimating how much power we really have," sighed Spiffo.

"Sam's right," added Johansson. "There's treaties, agreements and pacts that have been made at the international level. We are bound by those and if we break them there will be retaliation and punishment."

"You mean there's an international agreement to ban cash?"

"It's not written in those exact words but, yes, that's the gist of it."

"So, let me get this straight," said JJ. "If everything goes to plan today, Mr Spiffo stops his daughter from killing Todhammerstein and the congress finishes up without incident, nothing will change?"

"We're right back to square one," muttered Svenson.

"Maybe we should let Samantha kill Todhammerstein after all," suggested Krusty.

"No chance," said Spiffo. "I don't want her to live with that for the rest of her life."

"Then we're screwed."

"Look," said Johansson checking his watch. "Sam and I need to go and start getting ready for the congress. I will say this. Whoever came up with the idea of fighting Todhammerstein on ideological grounds was on the right track. Make him look like a fool or a hypocrite, show that his ideas are ridiculous, better yet, provide a better, more compelling vision than he does. That's how you can beat him."

"How can we do that in one day with no preparation?" moaned Krusty.

"I don't know. But if you find a way, Sam and I will support you in whatever way that we can. Now we're going to go and get ready. You've got your passes for the ceremony, right?"

"Yes," nodded JJ.

"Good. We'll see you there."

With that Johansson and Spiffo left the room. JJ sat down on a nearby chair.

"Well, that's it. We're fucked," said Krusty.

"It's funny," said Amber. "I always thought our problems could be solved through politics. But it turns out that's not the case."

"The political system is just a façade," said Svenson matter-of-factly. "An unnecessary hierarchical structure placed on top of self-organising entities who it convinces could not survive without it."

"Sounds right to me," added Macca. "I mean, this whole time we thought Macbeth was running the Corporation. But it was Snake. And even then he stabbed us in the back when it came to the crunch."

"So, if politics can't solve it, what can solve it?"

"We can," said JJ. "Like Johansson said, though, we'll have to do it ourselves."

"Do what, bro?"

"I've got an idea. But it's gonna sound a bit crazy."

"Crazier than anything else that has happened in the last week?"

"Maybe."

"Alright. Let's hear it."

"Before I tell you, let me ask you a question, Macca. How much dope is there stored at Macbeth headquarters?"

"About two weeks' supply for the whole of Sydney."

"How much is that exactly?"

"In technical terminology, a shitload."

"Alright. And how many Corporation members can we get there in say the next fifteen minutes?"

"If we call in a Code Red, I'd say more than a hundred."

"Good. So here's the plan. We call in a Code Red and we spend the next two hours rolling as many joints as we can. The final ceremony today is being held in the football stadium not far from here. If we hurry, I reckon we can roll enough joints for everybody in the crowd."

"What's that going to achieve?"

"It's like Johansson just said, we have to make Todhammerstein look ridiculous. If we can get the entire stadium stoned, they'll listen to what he says and realise it's a crock of shit."

"Ok, dude. That's officially the new dumbest idea I've ever heard," said Krusty. "It's even dumber than making Todhammerstein catch a cold."

"How are you going to get the crowd to smoke them?" asked Amber.

"That's the key part," said JJ. "I'll get Todhammerstein to smoke one first."

"How are you gonna do that?"

"Same thing we did at the taste test for the kale. We'll call it cough medicine just like we did with those judges. Like Krusty said, none of the people in the Global Council know what weed is. If Todhammerstein gets up and smokes a joint in front of the whole world, the façade will break down. Now, he might deny it later and say he thought it was cough medicine. Great. He looks like a complete idiot who doesn't know the difference between weed and cough medicine. Plus, half the people won't believe him and they'll think he's some big stoner who won't admit it. Either way, he looks like a fool and we win."

"Ok. But what's the point of getting everybody in the crowd to smoke a joint too?"

"Todhammerstein might try and worm his way out of it later by saying he was set up. But if everybody in the crowd is smoking, he won't be able to do that. Even if he tries, it will be an admission of fallibility. The leader of the world encouraging a whole stadium of people to get stoned and then admitting he was tricked. Whichever way you cut it, his façade of invincibility gets broken."

"It's probably just cos the last few days have been insane, but this plan actually sounds plausible to me," said Amber.

"Krusty? Whaddya reckon?"

"I still say it's the dumbest plan I've ever heard. But getting Todhammerstein and a stadium full of losers stoned sounds like fun. So, count me in, bro."

"Alright. Macca, call in the code red and let's get back to HQ and start rolling some joints."

Chapter 8

In the main room at Macbeth HQ, tables had been laid out end to end in a giant joint production line. The Code Red had been more successful than Macca anticipated and there were about a hundred and fifty leather clad dudes and dudettes lined up beside giant black plastic bags full of weed rolling their hearts out. It was the first time in his life Krusty was the best at something. The pile of joints in front of him towered above his next best rival. His superiority was mostly due to the fact that he could roll two joints at the same time, one in each hand. It was a technique he'd developed over a period of years and, combined with the muscle memory that only comes from hours and hours of practice, it now gave him an almost one hundred percent productivity edge. But productivity was increasing across the board as people got the hang of what they were doing. Even Amber, who had never rolled a joint in her life, was churning out about two a minute.

JJ had taken on the role as chief overseer ensuring that nobody on rolling duty ran out of weed and that rolled joints were swiftly packed away into the cardboard boxes that had been procured for that purpose. For a group of ruffians and mobsters, the Macbeth associates were surprisingly disciplined and responded to JJ's exhortations to roll as many joints as they could for the next two hours with the promise to get an entire football stadium of people stoned; a worthy goal in the eyes of all who were present.

At around two o'clock in the afternoon, JJ walked over to Macca to let him know that he, Krusty, Svenson and Amber would be leaving to go to the ceremony. He left instructions for Macca and the others to load as many joints as they could into the van and get as many members as they could to the stadium by three o'clock. JJ would organise with Johansson to have them allowed into the stadium where they were to walk around handing out one joint to each person in the crowd.

With preparations made, they jumped into the black van and Tommy drove them the short trip to the stadium with a quick stop at the park opposite 12 Alice Street so that JJ could retrieve their passes from the place he hidden them. The crowd which made its way through the turnstiles were dressed to the nines in suit and ties, the occasional bow tie and a number of frilly hats and gowns. It looked like a crowd at a Melbourne Cup horse race. JJ, Krusty and Svenson were still dressed in their North Shore outfits and Amber was in a floral dress. They were underdressed for the occasion but not so badly as to draw attention to themselves.

They made it through the gates of the stadium without incident and, based on the "elite" status of their passes, were escorted by an official into the area that had been specifically set aside for the Global Council members. There was another checkpoint to go through, however, this one manned by the familiar looking soldiers in full body armour with machine guns at the ready. But they made it through with a minimum of fuss and walked into the stadium. The bay where the Global Council members were sitting had been demarcated on all sides by large panes of what might have been either bullet proof glass or germ protector panels, or both. It was right behind where the goalposts would have been on the field below. Some seats at the front of the bay had been removed to create a kind of podium and there was a microphone on a stand were presumably Todhammerstein's big speech would be given. In the seats directly behind it were the Global Council members. There were about five rows of them altogether making up about one hundred people. JJ recognised the six judges from the taste testing who were seated in the second row back. In the middle of the first row, there were two seats empty. Johansson and Spiffo sat immediately to the right of them.

"There's two people missing," said JJ scanning the area. "The two most important people."

"Macbeth and Todhammerstein," said Krusty.

"You mean, Samantha," corrected Amber.

"Yeah. Her."

"Let's go and ask Spiffo if he knows where they are," said JJ.

They walked down the steps to the front row where Spiffo was talking to Johansson.

"Oh, you're here," said Johansson catching sight of them as they approached.

"We're here but where's Samantha and Todhammerstein?" asked Amber.

"We haven't been able to find out exactly where they are," said Johansson. "We do know that they're together, though."

"Oh, man. That means she's probably already infected him with the virus," said JJ.

"It doesn't look like it," said Johansson.

"Why?"

"Cos she's joining the Global Council," erupted Spiffo jumping out of his seat in a sudden rage. "I have a right mind to strangle Todhammerstein when I see him."

Spiffo cast about angrily with his fists clenched as if he really was going to do what he said.

"Settle down, Sam," said Johansson looking around nervously as several people in the area cast sideways glances in their direction. "You can't strangle him here, anyway. Those boys with machine guns won't let you."

"Whaddya mean she's joining the Global Council," asked Krusty.

"Todhammerstein has nominated Samantha as the Youth Ambassador for the Global Council. It's going to be announced shortly at the ceremony."

"Well, on the positive side, I guess that means she won't kill him," said Amber.

"Maybe she'll kill him after the announcement," suggested Svenson.

"Can't we stop this from happening? I mean, couldn't you talk her out of it, Mr Spiffo," asked JJ.

"I'll do more than talk her out of it. I'll carry her out of here if I have to."

"Sam, you've got to stay calm," said Johansson. "Talk to her rationally. We don't want to make a scene."

"Hang on, I just realised this creates a problem for us," said JJ.

"What?" asked Amber.

"If Samantha has joined the Global Council, that makes us the enemy now. Krusty, Svenson and me are supposed to be here to kill Todhammerstein. That's the deal I made with Samantha yesterday. If she sees us, she will probably assume that is what we are here to do and she might have us arrested or worse."

"You'll need to make sure Samantha doesn't see you then," said Johansson.

Suddenly the PA system of the stadium kicked into life with what sounded like a trumpet call followed by a voiceover person.

"Ladies and gentlemen, please rise for his Excellency, the leader of the Global Council, Professor Doktor Mr Kurt von Todhammerstein."

The crowd in the stadium stood up including the members of the Global Council who bowed in unison as Todhammerstein entered at the rear of the bay. By his side, dressed in a frilly black dress was Samantha Spiffo who surveyed the scene like a Queen might survey her subjects.

"Dudes, duck!" whispered Krusty to JJ and Svenson and they crouched down to ensure they would be unseen.

"Go over to the side. You should be safe over there out of sight," said Johansson pointing to a place in the rear corner of the bay.

They hurried over to the spot as inconspicuously as they could while Todhammerstein and Samantha made their way to the front row and took their seats in the centre like a king and queen receiving applause from the crowd. Halfway there, JJ realised he had forgot something. He ran back and whispered into Johansson's ear. Johansson called over one of his officials and gave him some instructions. JJ joined Krusty and the others at the back while the official scurried up the stairs and out of the bay.

"We will now commence the parade," announced the PA system and on the field below a military procession began featuring a marching band and a number of uniformed soldiers, sailors and air force personnel.

"Now's your chance," whispered Johansson to Spiffo. "See if you can pry Samantha away from Todhammerstein before the speeches."

Spiffo nodded and he and Johansson swapped seats so that Spiffo was sitting next to his daughter.

"Hello, Samantha," said Spiffo as he sat down.

Samantha turned her head ever so slightly with her face continuing to wear the faux-regal mask which showed no glimmer of familial recognition let alone affection.

"I'm afraid you have the wrong person. My name is Pickles Macbeth," she said coldly.

"Yes, I've heard all about your little extra curricular activities. You've been a busy girl with your Corporation, haven't you?"

Samantha didn't answered but continued to gaze onto the field as the military band kicked into a second tune.

"I also know about your little plan," said Spiffo in a low voice into his daughter's ear. "The one to assassinate the old man to your left."

"Oh, that? I changed my mind," said Samantha as if it was nothing.

"Oh, did you. Well that's just delightful."

"I have accepted a new role with the *old man* you refer to."

"So I hear. You're going to be a global ambassador."

"That will be the official title."

"And what will be the unofficial title?"

"I will also be a member of the Global Council."

"And what does that mean?"

"By joining the Global Council I can take my activities to the next level."

"By *activities*, I assume you are referring to graft, fraud and crime?"

Samantha shrugged.

"Samantha, I'm speaking to you now as the deputy Prime Minister and I'm telling you we will be shutting down your Corporation first thing tomorrow morning. It's against the law, you know."

"Pffft. The Global Council is above the law of Australia," said Samantha in a sing song voice.

"But your Corporation isn't."

"Soon the Corporation will be part of the Global Council. Therefore, it will be above the law."

"We'll see about that," said Spiffo who had been trying his hardest to control his temper but now broke out into his disciplinarian father voice. "You and I are leaving. C'mon."

Spiffo got up out of his seat. Samantha looked at him disdainfully.

"I'm not going anywhere."

"Oh yes you are."

Spiffo went to grab Samantha's wrist but she pulled her hand away.

"Guards!" she shouted and two armed guards standing nearby came over.

"What's the problem?" asked one of the them.

"This man is behaving inappropriately," said Samantha coldly.

"*This man*? I'm your bloody father," shouted Spiffo.

"C'mon, Sam, sit down," said Johansson getting up and putting his arm around Spiffo's shoulder to guide him back to his original seat. "It's ok, guards. Just a little misunderstanding."

Johansson took his seat next to Samantha while a still fuming Spiffo sat beside him.

From the back of the bay, JJ and the others had been watching the events unfold.

"That doesn't look good," said Amber as the guards returned to their initial position off to the side.

"I'm guessing Spiffo didn't talk Samantha out of it," said JJ.

"Let me go and find out," said Amber who got up and walked down to the front row where her father and Spiffo were seated.

She returned a few minutes later with the news.

"What happened?" asked JJ.

"Ok," said Amber taking a deep breath, "Samantha is joining the Global Council. She wants to take the Macbeth Corporation global."

"What?"

"Dude, that's fucked up."

"Can't Spiffo stop her? He is her father," asked JJ.

"He tried. She's a smart cookie, though. She knows how to get her way. That's what that business with the guards was all about. This means she won't be leaving. She'll be here for the speeches."

"Well, this has completely ruined my plan," said JJ.

"Why?" asked Krusty.

"I can't get Todhammerstein to smoke a joint with Samantha sitting right next to him. She'll rat me out to the guards."

"Not if you rat her out first."

"Whaddya mean?"

"Think about it, bro. Samantha was going to kill Todhammerstein. Snake said she had some kind of device on her to do the infecting. That means she probably still has the murder weapon with her."

"Even if that's true, I don't want to get her in trouble for that. Who knows, these guards will probably execute her."

"You don't have to, bro. You just have to threaten her. That should stop her from ratting you out."

"Mutually assured destruction," said Svenson.

"Huh?"

"It's the doctrine of mutually assured destruction. You can destroy Samantha and she can destroy you. This means it's in neither party's interest to fight. It's a basic concept of game theory."

"I'm not sure Samantha is up to date on the latest innovations from game theory," said JJ.

"She doesn't have to be. You just have to make it clear to her that you can destroy her as much as she can destroy you."

"What does all this mean?"

"It means we proceed as planned and you have to just deal with Samantha when you come to her."

"Look. They're here!"

Amber pointed across into the stadium and JJ and the others looked out through the clear plastic panes of the Global Council's bay to see figures in black making their way through the crowd. They were the tattooed and leather-clad Macbeth associates handing out joints to bemused people some of whom were holding them up to their noses and realising what they really were.

"Woah. It totally worked, dude. I can't believe it."

"Hey, there's Macca," said Svenson as the familiar large, bald tattooed figure gave a wave from about fifty metres away in the next bay.

"There's no turning back now, bro," said Krusty to JJ.

"Alright. I think I have a plan B," said JJ. "Amber, can you ask your father and Spiffo to come over here. We'll need their help."

"Ok," said Amber who hurried down the steps and whispered something to the two men who got up and followed her to the back.

"Alright, what's this plan of yours?" asked Johansson.

"Remember how you gave the judges at the taste test this cough medicine," said JJ holding up a joint so Spiffo could see it.

"You don't have to call it cough medicine," said Spiffo. "We know what marijuana is."

"What?" said JJ looking up in surprise. "So, you knew all along what was happening?"

"Of course, "said Spiffo. "We're not total dweebs like these Global Council members."

"So, why didn't you bust us?"

"Sometimes in politics it's better to keep information in your pocket for later use. Besides, those joints were exactly what was necessary to calm those judges down."

"Ok. Well, here's the plan. We want to get Todhammerstein to smoke a joint. In order to do that, we will keep pretending that this is cough medicine and offer it to the Global Council members. If we start with those three judges that have already smoked it, we'll have the best chance of success. Since they know and trust you both, I was hoping you could make the offer. It will make them more likely to accept."

"You want us to get the Global Council stoned?" asked Johansson.

"You said we had to win the ideology battle. That's what we're trying to do."

"How is this ideology?"

"I don't have time to explain. You said you would help us and this is what we need."

"It's fine," said Spiffo. "We'll do it. We need to try anything at this point and getting everybody stoned sounds like as good a plan as any."

"There's just one more thing I need to know," said JJ. "Does Samantha know what a joint is?"

Spiffo thought about it for a moment.

"I would say no. But, as you've probably figured out, I don't know my daughter anywhere near as well as I thought I did."

"Dude, she'd have to know what dope is. She's been running the Macbeth Corporation and it's one of their main lines of business."

"No. Snake was running the Macbeth Corporation. We know that Samantha wasn't actively involved."

"What does it matter if she knows?" asked Svenson.

"She's sitting right next to Todhammerstein. If we tell him it's medicine and she knows it's not, she could spoil the whole plan."

"Not if we neutralise her with mutually assured destruction."

"Mutually assured what?" asked Spiffo.

"Just leave it to us, bro," said Krusty. "We'll take care of Samantha and you target Todhammerstein."

"A classic pincer movement," said Svenson. "We'll take them from both sides."

"I'll go with Krusty and Svenson to help out," said Amber.

"Ok," said JJ. "Sounds like a plan. Now can everybody get out their joints, please."

Krusty, Svenson and Amber had all stashed a number of joints on their person in various hiding places where their clothing would allow it. Krusty in particular was a master of the technique and was pulling joints from all kinds of places until he had a handful which he gave to JJ.

"I need something to put them in," said JJ who looked around for a suitable container and found an empty cardboard drinking cup nearby.

He looked inside to check that it was dry and then began loading the joints in until eventually it looked something like the chamber of a six shooter although there were more than sixty bullets in this gun.

"Ok, everybody ready?"

"Let's do this, bro."

JJ led Johansson and Spiffo up and around the main seating area to the next aisle over and then back down til they were one row from the front where the judges from the taste test were sitting. The men were all dressed in tuxedos while the women were in formal gowns and hats to shield from the sun which was shining brightly above.

"Excuse me, ladies and gentlemen," said Spiffo in his most officious voice. "We thought you might like another dose of our cough medicine which you seemed to benefit from a couple of days ago."

JJ pulled a few joints out of the container and held them up so they could see what Spiffo was referring to.

"Oh, absolutely," gushed the female judge. "You know, I had the best night's sleep I've ever had after taking that medicine."

"It's true, ma'am," said JJ putting on his best salesman persona. "Although our medicine is primarily a cough medicine it has a number of other health benefits which we're only just discovering."

JJ held out the container and the judges took a joint each while encouraging those around them to also try the "wonder drug".

Meanwhile, on the other side of the bay, Krusty, Svenson and Amber headed down the aisle to the front row and, noticing that Todhammerstein was in conversation with the person sitting to his left, took up the seats to the right of Samantha where Johansson and Spiffo had been sitting. Amber and Svenson sat down while Krusty stood in front and waved for Samantha's attention.

"It's you," she said with a measure of consternation casting an eye over to Svenson and Amber sitting next to her.

"Surprise, bro. Remember us? We're the ones you tried to have knocked off."

"Where is Snake?"

"He's under arrest," said Amber. "He'll be charged with attempted murder among other things."

"You're lying."

"Oh, really? Then why are we here and he isn't?"

Samantha didn't respond. She just scowled in Krusty's direction with one eye on the nearby guards.

"We need one of those, errr, one of those fire devices," said the woman in the frilly hat.

JJ reached over and held up the lighter as the woman in the fourth row, copying the others she had seen do it before her, lit the joint between her lips and took a drag.

"Oooh," she said. "Interesting taste."

JJ repeated the process for two others nearby and then for several in the next row who had decided to try it out. One of them began spluttering immediately on lighting up.

"I thought this was supposed to be cough medicine," said a man in a tuxedo from the row behind who had been watching the proceedings.

"This is all part of the process," said JJ without missing a beat. "You may experience some coughing in the short term but over the long term coughing decreases substantially."

"He's right," agreed the lady judge from two rows down, who was becoming the main advocate for the medicine, "I haven't coughed once since I tried it the other day."

"Hmmm, alright. I'll try one," said the man.

"Me too," said the person sitting next to him and in short order the entire row was lighting up.

"One call to the guards and I'll have you all arrested in seconds," said Samantha.

"Try it, bro. We'll have you arrested too."

"Hah. How are you gonna do that?"

"We know about you're little device," said Svenson. "Snake told us about your plan to infect the old man."

"They won't believe you. I'm just a girl. And one that is about to be announced as a Global Ambassador. I'll be taking the Corporation global."

"No, you won't," said Amber. "The Corporation is finished."

"Check it out dude," said Krusty gesturing around the stadium. "See all those figures in black handing out things to the crowd? Look familiar? They're Macbeth associates. Hundreds of them, bro. All here to help us."

"And guess what?" added Svenson. "We told them all that you're Sam Spiffo's daughter. They know you've been faking all this time."

Samantha looked over into the stands to see for herself and her look of consternation disappeared and was replaced by something approximating rage.

".....oh, yes. It's the latest technological innovation from our scientists in the lab. Ground breaking stuff," said Spiffo who was quite enjoying using his rhetorical skills to con the Global Council members into smoking marijuana.

The take up had been almost universal and a cloud of white smoke developed which hung in the breezeless air of the stadium. There was only one row left to target: the front one.

"Anybody here like to try the newest cough medicine from our boys in the lab?" Spiffo asked.

"A smokable medicine?" asked the man in the aisle seat.

"It's designed for fast acting relief," said JJ. "A digested medicine can take up to an hour to have an effect while a medicine that is inhaled has an immediate effect."

"It certainly seems to be having an immediate effect on them," said the man gesturing to the second row where an outbreak of giggling had occurred.

"A mild state of euphoria is one of the pleasant side effects of the medicine," said JJ.

"Bus boy, we need some food over here. Bring some potato chips," shouted the woman in the third row.

"And some hamburgers," shouted another.

"Bring five buckets of chips too."

"As you can see, the medicine also stimulates the appetite," smiled JJ.

"Let me try it then," said the man in the front row who took a joint and make a credible effort to light it.

JJ looked on the scene before him. Todhammerstein was still talking to the man to his left. At each end of the row were a dozen fully armed guards. And in the middle was Samantha talking to Amber. There would be no escape from here on in.

JJ raised his eyebrows to Krusty to try and get a signal about whether things were looking good and Krusty waved his hand discreetly to say that it was. With Spiffo and Johansson bringing up the rear, JJ bypassed the people in the seats to his right and made his way directly for Todhammerstein.

"Excuse me, Mr Todhammerstein," said JJ looking again into the eyes of the man which seemed to him even colder and greyer than he remembered despite the bright sunshine of the day. "You might remember me from a couple of days ago. Paul Wochensky, the winner of the kale growing competition."

Todhammerstein gave the smallest of nods to indicate that he did.

"Mr Spiffo and I have just been handing out samples of our new cough medicine to your colleagues. As you can see, it's proving very popular. It's newly developed by myself and the others in the horticultural lab using the latest hydroponics science. I was wondering if you would you like to try it."

JJ held a joint out but before Todhammerstein could answer, Samantha swung herself around.

"Mr Todhammerstein, don't touch that!"

"What's the problem?" asked JJ.

"I think it might be poisoned," said Samantha.

"No way, bro," said Krusty. "Give it here and I'll prove it."

Krusty reached over and took the joint from JJ and lit it up taking an extra-long toke and breathing out a long plume of smoke.

"See? Not poison, at all."

"Besides," said JJ, "many of your colleagues are already trying it."

JJ waved to the female judge in the second row.

"Oh, it's absolutely the best," she called out with a mouth full of hamburger.

"But, I don't have a cough," said Todhammerstein.

"The medicine has a range of other health benefits including increased appetite, zest for life, relieves anxiety, encourages relaxation and benefits sleep," said JJ.

JJ pulled another joint out and held it up for Todhammerstein who took it and inspected it.

"Vat is in it?" he asked.

"It's a combination of the highest pharmaceutical grade components all manufactured in our laboratory," said JJ. "Allow me to start it for you so you can be sure that it is absolutely safe."

JJ took back the joint and flicked on the lighter which he held up to the end of the joint and inhaled enough to get it going. He handed it back to Todhammerstein who took a look at the people around to see how to do it then held the joint up to his lips and took a drag. He immediately broke out coughing.

"Don't worry. That just shows that it's working," JJ reassured him. "You should start off with small breaths first and move to larger ones once you get the hang of it."

Todhammerstein tried again and this time managed to inhale properly. JJ may have been imagining it, but it seemed that the man's facial features instantly softened. The hard wrinkles which held his face into a permanent frown seemed to loosen their grip. He took another toke on the joint and something resembling a smile took place on his face, although it was as if the smile muscles were being activated for the first time and didn't know how to work properly. The effect was disjointed and weird but it was still a smile. From the next seat over, Samantha scowled the scowl of a girl who knew something fishy was going on but couldn't figure out what it was.

"I want to try one," she demanded.

"The medicine is not normally recommended for children," said JJ. "Let's ask your father."

JJ turned theatrically to Spiffo who was standing beside him.

"Mr Spiffo, should we allow your daughter to try it?"

"Absolutely, not," said Spiffo in his best strict father voice.

Samantha crossed her arms and somehow managed to frown even more than she already was. She looked on as Todhammerstein took another toke.

"Zis is very good," he said. "Very good."

An official came scurrying down the row holding his hand up to get attention.

"Ladies and gentlemen, please take your seats. We are almost ready for the speeches," she said. "Prime Minister, are you ready?"

"Sure am," said Johansson.

"Excellent. We begin in about one minute."

Amber and Svenson got up to allow Johansson and Spiffo to sit down . The others moved down the row to the next aisle over and took a seat near the guards.

"Well, we've done all we can," said JJ. "It's in the hands of the gods now."

"Hey, who's the god of weed?" asked Krusty.

"Dionysus," said Svenson.

"Who?"

"Technically, there is no god of weed in western culture. But if there was, it would be Dionysus, the god of partying."

"Can you pray to Dionysus?"

"I think you just burn a joint in his honour."

"Done," said Krusty pulling a joint out of his pocket and lighting it up. "To Dionysus. May he smile upon us."

"Ladies and gentlemen, we will now hear the Prime Minister of Australia, Florian Johansson, introduce his Excellency, Kurt von Todhammerstein."

The voice over the PA reverberated around the stadium for a couple of seconds as Johansson got out of his seat and approached the microphone pulling out a piece of paper which he read from. On the big screen above, the camera that was pointed at the microphone also captured Todhammerstein in the background taking another giant toke of his joint and exhaling as if he'd been doing it for decades. Samantha sat with arms folded with an evil look on her face.

"Ladies and gentlemen, we are delighted to welcome you here today to celebrate the end of the congress of the Global Council which we have been honoured to host here in Sydney. As you can see behind me, we have been blessed to have all members of the Council here where we have charted a brave and exciting new course for the entire world. To introduce the new measures and explain what they signify for the future, I would like to introduce His Excellency, the Most Honourable and Exalted Grand Leader and Chief of the Global Council, Herr Professor Dr Mr Kurt von Todhammerstein."

Johansson returned to his seat and there was applause led enthusiastically by the members of the Global Council and followed by the crowd. The camera zoomed in ever so slightly on Todhammerstein who rose slowly to his feet and then promptly fell over sideways and backwards landing in the lap of the person on his left.

The crowd let out a gasp.

"He's been poisoned!" shouted Samantha jumping up from her seat. "Guards, arrest them."

The guards that were nearby surrounded JJ, Krusty, Svenson and Amber who were at the end of Samantha's pointed finger. Johansson got up and placed his hands in the air in a conciliatory tone.

"It's fine," he said. "It's fine. It's not poisoning. Mr Todhammerstein just lost his footing, that's all."

Johansson stepped over to help Todhammerstein back to his feet. In what was a horrifying spectacle that set everybody in the vicinity and those watching via the camera aghast, Todhammerstein was laughing, his mouth wide open revealing rows of yellowing teeth and gums with weird purple things on them.

"Why are you laughing?" asked Samantha crossing her arms in disapproval.

"Oh, my dear. I haven't had so much fun in my whole life."

"He's off his nut, bro," said Krusty taking another toke on his joint.

"Dionysus is working his magic," noted Svenson.

"See, Mr Todhammerstein is not poisoned," said JJ to the guards. "You can put the guns away now."

The lead guard looked across to see Johansson helping Todhammerstein over to the microphone and waved to the other guards to stand down. Meanwhile, Todhammerstein stood at the microphone leaning on Johansson's arm. He was looking not into the camera as might be expected, but up to the sky like a newborn baby seeing it for the first time.

"Vat a beautiful day it is here today. Ze sun is shining und ze birds are singing. Can you hear zem? I can hear zem."

Todhammerstein looked out at the audience who sat there is stunned silence as he held up the joint, which apparently he had kept hold of throughout his fall, and took a long toke before speaking again.

"I zscthink here in Sydney you have ze best of ze horticultural science what I have seen. Zis thing," Todhammerstein held up the joint to the crowd, "zis here is the latest in scientific research. A medicine formulated right here in Sydney. Zis is what ze science can do. It can make you happy and help to live a long and happy life."

Todhammerstein looked out blankly to the crowd as if he had forgotten where he was all of sudden.

"Vell, I vanted to say something else but I forgot," he said before breaking out into another burst of laughter. "Have a good day everybody."

With that, Todhammerstein turned around and Johansson helped him back into his chair where he sat down with a big smile on his face and took another toke of the joint.

Clearly the speech was meant to go for much longer and there were a couple of attendants frantically looking at each other to try and figure out what to do next. JJ saw his opportunity. He jumped up and walked over to the microphone.

"May I address the crowd very quickly?" he asked Todhammerstein.

"Yes, yes, my boy. Go," said Todhammerstein as if this was the greatest idea he had ever heard.

JJ stepped over to the microphone.

"Mr Todhammerstein would like to invite everybody to join him in enjoying this breakthrough technology," said JJ holding up a joint for the camera. "Everybody in the stadium should have a dose of the medicine which was handed out earlier. Please join us by getting a lighter from the nearest attendant. You start it like this."

JJ held his lighter up slowly and methodically so everybody could see. Among the crowd, the most common facial expression was bemusement as they pulled out what they knew to be a joint and waited for the lighters which were being handed out by the Macbeth Corporation associates or lit it up themselves if they had a lighter on them. Others, more innocent, seemed genuinely excited to be trying a new medicine. Up on the podium, and beamed throughout the stadium via the huge projector screens placed around, JJ handed the joint to Todhammerstein who inhaled like a pro and gave a big cheesy smile and a thumbs up for the camera. Behind him, members of the Global Council eagerly took up another dose and all around the stadium fast food sellers began to do a roaring trade as doughnuts, meat pies, hot dogs and chips were consumed at a frantic pace. A sweet smell permeated the air and a white haze softened the glare of the afternoon sun creating a shimmering atmosphere as joy and merriment broke out around the stadium and, with no speech to fill the allocated time, the camera simply panned around always returning back to the smiling face of one Kurt von Todhammerstein.

Epilogue

"JJ, hurry up. It's about to start," shouted Amber from the couch in the lounge room of the Johansson residence in Kirribilli.

JJ hurried in from the kitchen carrying a tray which had three bottles of beer and a gin and tonic on it. He held out the tray to Svenson and Krusty who took a beer each and then put it down on the coffee table where he picked up the gin and tonic and handed it to Amber before taking a seat beside her on the couch with his beer.

"To Dionysus," he said holding out the beer and they each clinked their drinks.

"Here we go, dudes," said Krusty holding up the remote and increasing the volume on the television. "We're on."

The opening credits faded away to show the news reader at her desk.

"Welcome to the six o'clock news, I'm Faye Daniels. In tonight's bulletin we will be giving extended coverage to the earthshattering changes that have occurred in Australian politics in the last twenty four hours. The parliament of Australia met for the first time in more than a decade today at the behest of Prime Minister, Florian Johansson. This came after a radical new agreement between Australia and the Global Council was signed by Mr Johansson and Kurt von Todhammerstein yesterday afternoon following the closing ceremony of the party congress in Sydney. Mr Johansson outlined the details of the deal at a press conference this morning."

The screen cut to footage of Johansson speaking into a microphone with Spiffo and a couple of others politicians behind him.

"We are proud to announce the signing of a new agreement between the Global Council and Australia. We worked around the clock yesterday afternoon to draft and present this agreement to Mr Todhammerstein before his flight back to Europe. I'll just give you the highlights for now. The new agreement renders all pre-existing agreements with the Global Council void and gives the parliament of Australia complete autonomy to set national policy from now on. Australia maintains all economic ties with the Global Council and we're delighted to announce that we have, at Mr Todhammerstein's explicit request, been granted preferred supplier status for pharmaceutical products with the Council. Our thanks go to Mr Todhammerstein and the entire Global Council for a negotiating a wonderful agreement."

"Haha, that's cos he was stoned off his head," laughed Krusty.

"They all were," added Svenson.

"Best time to negotiate," smiled Amber.

"How many joints did Todhammerstein burn through?" asked JJ.

"More than ten in the end," said Amber.

"That's an impressive effort for a first time smoker, dude."

"Deputy Prime Minister, Sam Spiffo, also praised the agreement and said that he looked forward to a new and improved working relationship with Mr Johansson and the parliament," said the announcer.

The camera crossed to an interview with Spiffo.

"Mr Johansson and myself have had our working difficulties in the past but the events of the last week have really brought us closer together. We realised we shared a number of things in common and one of them is a vision for an independent

Australia and I look forward to working with the Prime Minister to make that happen."

"Mr Johansson and Mr Spiffo announced a number of measures passed by the parliament with immediate effect. These included the removal of the cash bans across the nation meaning that all businesses will once against be able to accept physical currency for payment. The government will also cease all monitoring of electronic funds transfers as well as all other surveillance measures. All restrictions on the movement of people are to be lifted immediately and city walls will be demolished at the earliest possible opportunity."

"Sweet as, bro. We'll be able to travel to the city like normal again."

"And I'll be able to travel to Tittybong," said Amber leaning over and giving JJ a kiss on the cheek.

"There was controversy, however, surrounding another measure announced today which was the temporary nationalisation of the organisation known as the Macbeth Corporation. The Corporation, known to be Australia's largest underground network, has links to the Deputy Prime Minister's daughter and opposition MPs have accused the government of a coverup in relation to its activities. Deputy Prime Minister Spiffo countered this claim stating that the ringleader of the Corporation, known only as Snake, had been charged with numerous crimes and was due to be brought to trial within months. Meanwhile, the government announced that the nationalisation was only a temporary move and the Corporation would be broken up into a series of cooperative enterprises to be run by its employees in what may signal a brand new economic direction for the nation."

"Yeah, mate. I've got my eye on the transportation vertical myself," said Macca still dressed in full leather outfit and with his Macbeth tattoo showing prominently on his bare bicep as the news camera panned in for a closeup on his face.

"The Macbeth Corporation has been providing reliable service to customers for a number of years," said Tommy who was standing next to Macca, "and it was mostly run by employees anyway so we reckon it'll be a pretty easy transition to running the business ourselves as a co-op."

"Finally, the departure of Kurt von Todhammerstein was disrupted yesterday evening as the leader of the Global Council was threatened by an unidentified man at the Sydney airport."

The screen cut to shaky footage captured on a mobile phone which showed Svenson being held back by a number of security operatives while Todhammerstein made his way through the gates at the airport.

"Eyewitness reports say the man challenged Mr Todhammerstein to a duel while security personnel confiscated two swords at the scene. Police are believed to have later released the man without charge."

"Bro, you didn't get your revenge on Todhammerstein."

"On the contrary, failure to engage in a duel when challenged is an admission of defeat and brings shame on the entire family line of the Todhammersteins. My ancestral liability has been discharged," said Svenson.

"Well, that's good to know. Dude, they didn't say what was gonna happen with Macbeth's dope operations."

"I guess that's not the sort of thing they would talk about on the six o'clock news," said JJ.

"Amber, can you ask your old man next time you see him to find out what the deal is?"

"I think he's got more important things to worry about at the moment," said Amber.

"Hey, do you think we'll still be running the money supply in Tittybong?"

"No. I'm pretty sure the banks will do that from now on."

"So, what are we gonna do, dude?"

"You can go back to selling Krusty's Special," said JJ. "You might have to find some new middlemen, though."

"And what are you gonna do?"

"Dunno. Hang out here in sunny Kirribilli with the rich and powerful."

"Hah," said Amber giving JJ a whack on the arm. "You'll have to get a job too, now."

"Maybe you can run a co-op like Macca and Tommy," suggested Svenson.

"Hey, we should totally start our own co-op. We'll call it Krusty and Co. Whaddya reckon?"

"It's got a certain ring to it," said JJ.

"You don't seem too bothered either way, bro."

"Well, if there's one thing that last couple of weeks have taught me, it's that anything can happen," smiled JJ who put his arm around Amber and took another swig of his beer.

Note to the Reader

If you've made it this far, you've no doubt finished the whole book. Congratulations (I hope!).

Please consider leaving a review on your favourite book review website (eg. Goodreads, Amazon). Every review, positive and negative, is a big help.

Also by the Author

Once Upon a Time in Tittybong

JJ's best mates, Krusty and Trish, are hardcore, dyed-in-the-wool potheads. They're fun to have around. But sometimes, when you hang out with stoners too long, you do silly things like ask the Mayor if you can start a local currency that's backed by marijuana. Sometimes, when you live in the small Victorian town of Tittybong, the Mayor says 'Yes'.

Now JJ's going to spend his school holiday living the dream of every entrepreneurial high school stoner: running a bank where the money is made from dope. But the local manager of the State Bank, the leader of the local bikie gang and the local constabulary don't take too kindly to having their turf encroached on and JJ's about to find out that high finance is not all beers and bucket bongs.

Once Upon a Time in Tittybong is a fast-paced comedy in which a group of idealistic teenagers take on the powers that be in an Australian country town.

Narquinxa and Xandalus

Narquinxa never wanted to visit planet Earth. There were some nice trees and stuff but the so-called intelligent life form known as human beings weren't very impressive by inter-galactic standards. But she had a job to do. A job that was made harder when her boss partnered her with that idiot, Xandalus. Their mission: get themselves a couple of bodies, drop down to Earth for a few days and investigate the humans.

It should have been straightforward but Xandalus did more than investigate; he fell in love with a human female. Narquinxa could have slapped him for his stupidity. But then she started to fall in love too. Just when they were both thinking that Earth wasn't so bad after all, Xandalus did the one thing he had been explicitly instructed not to do and helped the humans create some new technology. Not just any technology; artificial intelligence. When the AI falls into the hands of a psychopathic army officer, Narquinxa must save not just her bumbling partner, but the entire human race from destruction.

An inter-galactic love story set in Melbourne, Australia, Narquinxa and Xandalus is equal parts action, sci fi, and comedy.

If Douglas Adams wrote a romance novel, it might look a little like this.

The Order of the Secret Chiefs

"Sampson, you've got a woman problem."

Adam Sampson does indeed have a woman problem: a sexy Russian witch has taken over his apocalypse cult (it's a long story). Fortunately, Adam has help from his pickup artist mate, Liam Love, and spunky grandmother, Mrs Mitchell. Together, the three of them will have to fight to stop Madame Orlova and her horde of horny men from bringing about the end of the world.

The Order of the Secret Chiefs is a riotous action-comedy in which a young man gets in over his head with money, sex and magic. His fight to save the world will be the beginning of his journey of self discovery in life and in love.

www.ingramcontent.com/pod-product-compliance
Lightning Source LLC
Chambersburg PA
CBHW070012120726
47909CB00003B/903

* 9 7 8 0 6 4 8 9 4 8 6 5 0 *